D0974793

FROM
ABOVE

FROM ABOVE

NORAH McCLINTOCK

ORCA BOOK PUBLISHERS

Library and Archives Canada Cataloguing in Publication

McClintock, Norah, author
From above / Norah McClintock.
(Riley Donovan)

Issued also in print and electronic formats.
ISBN 978-1-4598-0933-8 (pbk.).—ISBN 978-1-4598-0934-5 (pdf).—
ISBN 978-1-4598-0935-2 (epub)

I. Title.
PS8575.C62F75 2016   jc813'.54   C2016-900548-8
C2016-900549-6

First published in the United States, 2016
Library of Congress Control Number: 2016933648

Summary: In this mystery for teen readers, Riley Donovan uncovers the
truth about the death of a popular high school football player.

*Orca Book Publishers is dedicated to preserving the environment and has
printed this book on Forest Stewardship Council® certified paper.*

Orca Book Publishers gratefully acknowledges the support for
its publishing programs provided by the following agencies:
the Government of Canada through the Canada Book Fund and the
Canada Council for the Arts, and the Province of British Columbia
through the BC Arts Council and the Book Publishing Tax Credit.

Cover design by Teresa Bubela
Cover photography by iStock.com

ORCA BOOK PUBLISHERS
www.orcabook.com

Printed and bound in Canada.

19 18 17 16 • 4 3 2 1

Also by Norah McClintock

ONE

A damp, dreary day was made drearier by Ashleigh's lateness. Where was she? She should have been here ages ago. I glanced at the clock on the wall. Okay, she should have been here five minutes ago. But it wasn't as if this was some last-minute thing she might have forgotten. She had been meeting me every day after class since school began. We did our homework together on the days she wasn't working. I walked her to the grocery store on the days she was. That meant I never had to walk past Mike Winters' locker alone.

Mike's locker was the first one at the top of the stairs. He was always there after school, and it took him forever to get his stuff together. I'd never seen a guy take so long. It meant that I couldn't leave—okay, so I *refused* to leave—okay, okay, so I was *afraid* to leave—without having someone like Ashleigh leave with me. I realize how that makes me sound. But it's the truth.

Get over it, I told myself. What had happened, happened. It was history now. Besides, everything had turned out okay, hadn't it? Sure, I'd accused Mike of terrible things. But I'd done it in good faith. I'd believed what I said at the time that I said it. It might be a lame defense, but it's also the truth.

"Boo!"

I jumped and spun around, my heart pounding. Ashleigh.

"Are you still here?" She seemed surprised.

"Of course I'm still here. I was waiting for you. Remember?"

"In that case, you're lucky I came this way." When she saw the blank look on my face, she shook her head. "You forgot, didn't you?"

"*Me*? You're the one who forgot. We meet here at the same time every day."

"Except for today. I told you, Riley. It's picture day."

"What?" Picture day? Today? "When? Now?"

Ashleigh was right. I had forgotten. Otherwise I would have paid more attention to my hair. I would have dressed differently. There was no way I wanted to appear in my first-ever school yearbook with a greasy mop of hair and a pilled sweater that was the first warm thing I'd grabbed this morning. I blamed Mr. Jespers. If he hadn't given us a ridiculous assignment—a multimedia presentation that expressed our individuality—I wouldn't have stayed up half the night editing old videos together with music that was important to me. I would have gotten up in time to attend to my personal hygiene. I rooted in my backpack for my brush and wished I'd stuck a mirror to the inside of my locker the way most of the other girls had done.

And I cursed school. I'd never liked the idea of it. I definitely did not enjoy the practice of it. When I'd lived with my grandpa Jimmy, which I had for most of my life, school had consisted of distance education via computer. That's because Jimmy had been constantly on the road with his rock group, which had had half a dozen hit songs before I was born. When Jimmy died, I had been shipped off to live with Aunt Ginny, my mother's younger sister. Her father, my grandpa Dan, took over my education for a while. But a couple of months back, Aunt Ginny had been offered a plum job, and we'd moved to Moorebridge. Result: I was forced to enrol in school.

"Relax," Ashleigh said. "It's not *that* picture day. It's National Student Photography Day. Hey, what happened to your four-leaf clover?"

"What?" I looked at the small fabric loop on my backpack where the green-and-gold clover had hung ever since Charlie had given it to me for my fifteenth birthday. *So your year will be filled with good luck,* he'd said. But the clover was gone. I scanned the floor frantically.

"Maybe it fell off in your locker," Ashleigh said.

I searched it thoroughly. The clover wasn't there.

"It could be anywhere." I moaned. "I don't even know how long it's been missing."

"I'd help you look, but like I said, it's—"

"—National Student Photography Day. What is that anyway?"

"You didn't listen to me at all, did you?" She let out a dramatic sigh and rattled off a description that I had to admit sounded vaguely familiar. "It's a contest. Students right across the country participate. There's a theme every year. And the rule is that everyone has to take their picture on the same day at the same time—no cheating. There are great prizes—cash and cameras."

"And you're participating?" It was amazing how much I didn't know about my best friend. I'd had no idea at all that Ashleigh was interested in photography. In my defense, Ashleigh and I had met a mere two months ago, when I moved here with Aunt Ginny.

"You bet I am. I came fourth in the regionals last year. I won a great camera." She dug in her backpack and produced it. "Digital, but professional quality." She glanced at the clock above the bank of lockers. "I really have to go. We only have two hours to get the perfect shot."

"What's the theme?"

"From above."

"From above what?"

She grinned. "From above whatever you decide. One guy I know ditched his afternoon classes so he can be on the top of Bald Mountain in time to try to get a shot of the eagle's nest up there."

"There are eagles on Bald Mountain?" That was news to me.

"One girl is going to photograph lake life from the surface. You know, from above."

"That'll be fun in the rain," I said. It had started drizzling while I was riding to school. The drizzle had turned into a downpour, which had eventually slowed to a steady shower that continued all day. I wasn't looking forward to the wet ride home.

"Look out a window," Ashleigh said. "The rain stopped fifteen minutes ago. The sun is out. And FYI, Mike pulled some strings with one of his uncles to get permission to go up on the water tower and get some panorama shots that he wants to turn into one picture of the whole town."

"Mike *Winters?*" The same Mike whose cutting glances I had been dodging for weeks? "Mike Winters competes in photography contests?"

"I know he doesn't seem like the type. But he's good," Ashleigh said. "You wouldn't ever guess it, because he can be such a jerk. But put a camera in his hands and he's a different person. He has an eye for a great shot. I heard him tell someone else in the camera club that he likes the way things look through a lens."

"What does that mean?"

"I have no idea. But wait till you see my entry." She stowed her camera in her pack. "Gotta run." She raced down the hall, leaving me to contemplate the notion of Mike Winters' artistic eye. She was right. I never would have guessed.

I rolled up my rain poncho, stuffed it in my backpack and went boldly down the stairs and out the front door.

My bike was locked up at the recreation center next door to Lyle Murcheson Regional High School. Unlike the school, the rec center had proper bike stands. On my way there, I scanned every square inch of wet and puddled ground, hoping to spot something twinkling in the afternoon sun. Something like, say, a green-and-gold four-leaf clover. But the only sparkling items I saw were wadded-up gum wrappers and a nickel. I had to find that charm. Charlie was already mad at me for something that wasn't my fault. Now he was going to think I'd ditched his gift on purpose.

I didn't find Charlie's clover in the schoolyard, so I kept my eyes on the ground as I walked slowly behind the almost-brand-new rec center, praying that I'd find the charm before I reached the bike stands. Then I heard what can only be called a blood-curdling scream.

The scream was followed almost instantly by a chorus of other, higher-pitched shrieks. At first I thought it was from some ridiculous girl drama. You wouldn't believe what the girls at my school screech about—everything from a new episode of their favorite TV show to the release of a movie starring the newest, hottest actor. It was pathetic. So when I heard all that yowling, I rolled my eyes.

Until someone shrieked, "Call an ambulance!"

Ambulance equals serious. I ran toward the commotion and found a clutch of girls in cheerleader uniforms, which explained the girly squealing. No one screams louder than a cheerleader. Put a squad of them together, and it's hyper-banshee time. These cheerleaders were huddled on the pavement behind the rec center, where, I guess, they had decided to practice, given the squishiness of the school athletic field. But the squad wasn't practising fan-thrilling cheers.

Most of them weren't even moving. Instead, they were frozen to the spot and staring at the ground. At something *on* the ground. Correction. At some*one*. I saw his—judging from the size of the shoes—sneakered feet first. The toes pointed to two o'clock and ten o'clock. I couldn't see his face right away, but from the way some girls were crying and others were moaning *ohmygawd, ohmygawd, ohmygawd*, it was clear not only that something bad had happened but also that they knew the person to whom it had happened.

The nearest cheerleader must have sensed an outsider, because she turned to me and clutched my arm. "Do you have a phone?"

I reached around to the side pocket of my backpack, extracted my cell phone and elbowed my way to the front of the cluster of girls. I wished I hadn't.

Ethan Crawford, one of Lyle High's standout athletes, was spread-eagled face up on the pavement, his thickly lashed hazel eyes staring up at where the breaking clouds were shifting slowly across the sky. He didn't blink. He couldn't. He wasn't breathing. How could he, with all that blood pooled on the ground under his head?

I punched 9-1-1 into my phone. While I waited for an answer, I looked up. Where Ethan was lying—not far from the base of a wall, feet closest to the wall, head farthest from it—as well as how he was lying—on his back, arms and legs outstretched—made me think he had fallen from above. I looked up. The sun chose that moment to break through the thinning cloud. It blinded me, and I raised a hand to shield my eyes. When I did, I caught a glimpse of someone on the roof of the rec center. At least, I *thought* that was what it was. A head and shoulders. A cheerleader grabbed my arm.

"Ambulance!" she screamed. "He needs an ambulance."

I looked up again. Whoever had been there was gone.

The 9-1-1 operator answered, and the training Aunt Ginny had drilled into me kicked in. I told her there was a teenage boy lying on the asphalt at the back of the recreation center in Moorebridge. "I don't think he's breathing," I added, even though I could see that he wasn't.

"Is anyone doing CPR?" the operator asked.

"No."

"Do you know how to do it?"

"Yes." Everyone on Jimmy's tour bus, including me, had taken regular CPR and first-aid refresher classes. Jimmy had insisted on it. *Just in case*, he had said.

"Then do it now," the operator said. "And stay where you are. Don't touch anything except the victim, and don't let anyone else touch anything. An ambulance is on its way."

I ended the call, shooed the gaggle of cheerleaders away from the body on the ground—I mean, the *person*. Ethan. They backed up a little but refused to leave, which was probably good because I had no doubt a police car would arrive along with the ambulance, and the cops would want to question everyone.

An ambulance arrived quickly. Moorebridge is a smallish place, although it's the biggest town in the county, home to the regional high school, the regional hospital and the regional police service. It's also the seat of county government and the home of all county-related jobs. The hospital is five minutes from the high school if you stick to the speed limit. The ambulance hadn't.

One of the paramedics asked if anyone had seen what happened. One girl said in a shaky voice that right after the cheerleading squad had started practicing, she'd thought she heard something hit the ground "like a sack of sand." She'd seen something out of the corner of her eye. At first she thought she was looking at a pile of old clothes. It took her a few seconds to make out a hand. She'd gone to investigate. She sounded stunned, as if she didn't believe what had happened. The other paramedic nudged me out of the way and knelt beside Ethan. He looked somber when he listened to Ethan's heart. He radioed his dispatcher and reported that all vital signs were absent and Ethan had what looked like severe head trauma and other trauma-related injuries. A moment later he covered Ethan and herded everyone back several more meters.

The first police car arrived. It seemed to have taken forever, although it was probably only ten minutes. A uniformed police officer got out. I didn't recognize him. He consulted with the paramedics and started separating witnesses (the cheerleaders) from the small crowd that had gathered with them. They pointed me out, and he shepherded me into the small herd of girls, shuffled us away from the body and told us to stay put until someone took our statements.

Then he started in on crowd control, urging the bystanders—a smattering of high-school-age kids and adults—to step back and, preferably, move along. *Nothing to see here, folks.* Another squad car pulled up and disgorged two more uniforms. They began to establish a perimeter around the scene with trestles and crime-scene tape.

Next came the plainclothes cops. Them I recognized—Detectives Martin and McFee. They stepped into the taped-off perimeter and spoke first to the paramedics. Then they examined the body without moving it. When they finished, Detective McFee looked around. Her eyes lit on me, but she didn't betray any sign of knowing me. I tried not to take it personally. That's just the way Aunt Ginny is—professional to the nth degree. Her boss scanned the crowd too. He is actually Detective *Sergeant* Martin, but I've never heard anyone call him that. Most people call him Josh. Either that or just plain "Detective." His reaction to seeing me there was decidedly unprofessional, if you ask me. He shook his head slowly, as if he wasn't at all surprised to find me in proximity to trouble and would be even less surprised if I turned out to be involved in or, better yet, guilty of whatever had happened.

Now that they had finished their preliminary look at the scene, Aunt Ginny and Detective Martin turned their attention to the witnesses. They started with the cheerleaders.

When Aunt Ginny finally released the last of the squad, she squared her shoulders and prepared to deal with me. Detective Martin thrust out an arm to bar her way. No way was he going to let her question her troublemaking (in his opinion) niece. He wanted that job himself.

He came at me, notebook in hand.

"Riley."

"Detective."

"I hear you were the person who called this in."

"That's right. None of them had a phone handy." I nodded at the cheerleaders, who were standing around on the fringes of the field as if not sure what to do next. A uniformed officer finally guided them through the trestles and under the black-and-yellow tape.

"I don't suppose you saw what happened." From his weary tone, I guessed this was supposed to be a rhetorical question.

"No, I didn't."

He sighed. Relief? Exasperation? I couldn't tell.

"What can you tell me about what happened?" he asked.

"I'd just left school. I was walking over to the bike racks at the rec center. I heard screaming," I said. "I went to check it out, and I saw the cheerleading squad. They were clustered together right there." I pointed to where Ethan was still lying, covered now against prying eyes and the elements. "They were standing around Ethan."

"So you know the victim?"

"Sort of. We go to the same school."

"What, if anything, do you know about what happened?"

"Nothing." I hesitated for a second before adding, "Except that I think there was someone else on the roof."

"Someone else? You mean someone other than Ethan?"

I nodded. "I looked up, and I'm pretty sure I saw someone up on the roof."

"Pretty sure?"

"The sun came out. It was hard to get a good look. At first I thought it was a mirage or something."

I kicked myself as soon as the words were out of my mouth. Detective Martin lowered his pen.

"A mirage. I see."

"But it wasn't a mirage," I said quickly. "There was someone up there."

"Can you describe this person? Was it someone you know?"

"No. I mean, I don't know if I know him because I didn't actually see who it was. Because of the sun. It was right behind him and—"

"You keep saying *him*. So it was a male?"

"He or she," I said. "It could have been a she. I couldn't tell."

"Did this person you think you saw say anything? Did you hear something? Is that why you looked up?"

"No. Nothing like that. I just didn't want to look at Eth—at the victim. So I looked up and I thought I saw—I mean, I did see someone."

"But you're not sure," Detective Martin said. "Because the sun was in your eyes." He scribbled a few quick notes and flipped his notebook shut. "If you think of anything else, you know how to reach me."

The coroner came and went, the body was bagged and taken away, and a uniformed officer told me what I assumed he had already told the cheerleaders—that I should report to the police station to make a formal statement. Aunt Ginny and Detective Martin left the scene. The cheerleaders huddled on the other side of the barricade for a few minutes before finally deciding to abort their practice. I headed to where I'd been going in the first place—the bike lockup. When I got there, the rec center's parking lot was filled with kids in brightly colored rain gear, and teachers and parents, most of them clutching furled umbrellas. They were making their way to school buses or family cars to go home after what a banner over the front rec-center door proclaimed as the *Annual Regional Swim Meet*. There seemed to be some kind of buzz among the adults. They stood or walked in small knots and kept glancing at the police cars at the far end of the building.

I unlocked my bike and set off for home, the image of Ethan's body flashing like a strobe light in my brain. I couldn't believe it had happened. I couldn't shake the picture of him staring up but seeing nothing. I couldn't believe he was dead.

A truck horn bellowed, and a massive dump truck screeched to a stop in the middle of an intersection. Its baseball-capped driver yelled at me to "Look at the light, for the love of Mike!" I did and saw to my horror that it was red. I had ridden through a red light.

I mumbled an apology and set off again, legs trembling. I was assiduous in watching for lights and stop signs—and trucks. So assiduous that I didn't see an elderly man open his car door in front of me. I managed to stop short without hurting myself or the car. But I startled the man so badly that he clutched his chest. I thought he was going to keel over. He didn't. Instead he shouted, "Watch where you're going, for Pete's sake!"

Then I heard, "Hey, Riley!"

It was Charlie. Where had he come from?

He grabbed my handlebars.

"Are you okay?" He peered at me, frowning.

"I'm fine." I was, too, if you overlooked the fact that I was shaking all over. I had just had a close call with first a truck and then a car door. It was pure luck that I wasn't sprawled on the pavement—just like Ethan.

"You don't look fine," Charlie said. "Plus, you almost ran someone over. That's not like you."

That's when I did what I hardly ever do. I burst into tears.

TWO

"What is it?" Charlie asked. "Are you hurt?"

"It's Ethan." I wiped my tears with the back of my hand.

"Oh." Bye-bye, sympathy and concern. Hello, disdain.

Charlie didn't like Ethan. There could have been any number of reasons for this. After all, both were born and raised in Moorebridge, which meant they'd had plenty of time to inflict pain on and nurse grudges against each other. That was my theory. Ashleigh had a different one: Charlie didn't like Ethan because, for some reason I hadn't figured out, Ethan had started hanging around me.

"So what happened?" Charlie's tone was mocking. "Did Mr. Wonderful decide to go back to his girlfriend?"

This was something else I was having trouble fathoming. Charlie acting obnoxiously jealous. Of Ethan. Okay, so yes, Ethan had been trailing me for the past week. And, yes, he'd dumped his girlfriend, Serena, just before he started mooning around my locker. But he hadn't asked me out, and even if he had, I'm not sure I would have accepted. For one thing, I didn't know him well. I had no idea what kind of person he was. For another, Serena gave the evil eye to every girl Ethan so much as glanced at. And if there's one thing I know—mostly because the guys in Jimmy's band told me every time they did what they subsequently warned me against—it's that it's never a good idea to get involved with someone who's fresh off a breakup. You need to give it time. A lot of time.

Not that any of this was even remotely relevant to my relationship with Charlie. We were friends. If that had changed, no one had told me.

"Oh, Charlie," I said. "Ethan's dead."

Charlie laughed. He actually laughed. I was furious. I tried to shake him loose from my handlebars. That's when I noticed his hand. I didn't have a chance to ask him about it, though, because he said something that made me even angrier.

"Yeah right. As if my dreams ever come true."

How could he be so cruel?

"I'm not kidding, Charlie. He's really dead."

"Nice try, Riley. But he was at school today, as charming as ever. I should know."

"You don't understand. It really happened. Just now. The cops were there. He's dead."

Doubt overtook Charlie's face. "You're not kidding, are you?"

"I was there. I saw him." It was as if I'd stumbled on the words of a malevolent spell. As soon as I spoke them, I saw Ethan again, eyes open, body motionless, lying in a pool of blood. I felt myself tremble.

"What happened?" Charlie asked. "How did—"

"He fell off the rec-center roof. You know, where the jocks like to hang out." There was a large patio on the roof that was used in the warm months for fresh-air yoga classes, seniors' exercise programs and other outdoor activities. The school jocks—mainly the football team—liked to take weights out there and work their biceps, triceps, quads, glutes and every other muscle in their bodies except, as far as I could tell, their brains.

"He fell?"

"I think he might have been pushed."

"What? What makes you think that?"

"I'm pretty sure I saw someone up there. Right after we found Ethan."

"We?"

I filled him in on what had happened since I'd parted company with Ashleigh.

"This person you saw," Charlie said. "Did you get a good look at him?"

I had to admit—again—that I hadn't.

"What did the cops say?"

"What they always say. Nothing."

"Maybe he jumped," Charlie said.

I gave him a sharp look. "Is that supposed to make me feel better? Because it doesn't."

Charlie mumbled a barely audible "Sorry."

"I have to get home." I waited for Charlie to let go of my handlebars. That's when I got another look at his hands. The knuckles of the right one were red. Some of them were skinned almost raw. "What happened? Were you in a fight or something?"

He whipped his hand out of sight behind his back. "I fell."

I looked at his other hand. There wasn't a mark on it. He would have had to fall on the knuckles of one hand to get the injuries I had seen. I was about to press him for details when his eyes shifted to my backpack. What if he noticed that his four-leaf clover was no longer attached to it?

"I'll see you tomorrow." I jumped onto my bike and shot down the street.

My cell phone buzzed before I'd gone very far. I stopped and checked it. Ashleigh had texted. **Did you hear what happened?**

I texted her back. **Where are you?**

I found her nursing a giant latte at a table in the window of the Sip 'n' Bite. "So I can keep an eye on what's happening," she explained. She nodded at the police station, which was kitty-corner to the café.

"What about the photo contest?"

"Done." She kept her eye on her target. I glanced across the street.

"Seen anything?"

"Not so far. You want my opinion? I bet it was suicide."

"Suicide? He didn't seem depressed to me."

"He was an athlete. And a guy. He hid his emotions. What if he was secretly pining for Serena?"

"Why would he pine for her? *He* dumped *her*, not the other way around."

"Technically," Ashleigh said, "Serena engineered the breakup." She took a tiny sip of her latte. Ashleigh was a slow drinker. It could take her nearly an hour to get through a mug that size. It never bothered her that the coffee went cold.

"Technically?" I asked. "And what do you mean she *engineered* it?"

"Serena was fed up with the way Ethan was acting. She told him he'd better change or else. That's when he said if she didn't like the way he was, then she was free to break up with him. She called him on it. She said she didn't like it. He said, *Fine, then I guess we're through*."

"In other words, he broke up with her."

"In other words, she said change or else. He refused to change, leaving her with no option but to act on the *or else*—in other words, to initiate breakup proceedings.

That's what makes it a technicality. It also makes her smart—really, she broke up with him, but he gets all the blame and she, therefore, gets all the sympathy." She said this with frank admiration, as if Serena had invented some devilishly clever new chess move.

"I don't think Ethan jumped off a roof over that," I said. "Like I said, he didn't seem depressed. Besides, if he didn't want to lose Serena, all he had to do was change whatever was bothering her."

Ashleigh seemed reluctant to let go of her theory.

"What do you think happened?" she asked. "Do you think it was an accident?"

"If only."

"What do you mean?"

I told her the same thing I had told Charlie. "I saw someone else on the roof."

"You think someone *pushed* him?"

"At the very least, the person I saw knows something."

"Maybe whoever it was went up there after Ethan jumped."

"He didn't jump. And the person on the roof didn't come down when he saw what had happened. Or when the police showed up. Why not?"

"Maybe he was freaked out by seeing a dead body."

"Maybe."

"Hey," she said after a brief silence. "What if the person you saw was Serena? What if she pushed him?"

"Why would she do that? You just told me she dumped him. Why would she push him off a roof if she'd already cut him out of her life?"

Ashleigh looked at me incredulously. "Are you kidding? The green-eyed monster. Jealousy."

"Uh-huh. And who exactly is she jealous of?"

"You. The minute Ethan was free of her, he started puppy-dogging you. Maybe she suspected that was the reason he broke up with her."

"Whoa. Time out. I thought *she* broke up with *him*. That technicality thing."

"Whatever. Even though she started the whole thing, I'm pretty sure what she wanted was for him to change, not walk away. Oh, and then there's Andes."

Andes, I had learned by the end of the first week of school, was a fullback on the football team. His real name was Andrew Maracle, but he was built like a mountain and could stop anything up to and including a Mac truck (it was said), so everyone called him Andes.

"Then there's Andes what?" I asked.

"As a suspect. If Ethan was pushed. Maybe Andes did it."

"What does he have against Ethan? They're on the same team. And it's not even like they're in competition with each other. They play completely different positions."

"Andes has a thing for Serena. Maybe he thought he'd finally score when Ethan broke up with her. I saw them together the other day."

"Serena and Andes?"

She nodded. "Maybe Ethan was having second thoughts about breaking up with Serena, and Andes didn't like that. Or maybe Serena was having second thoughts about breaking up with Ethan, and Andes decided to get rid of him before Serena tried to patch things up."

"That's a lot of maybes. Here's another one— maybe you should write a book. You have a pretty wild imagination."

"I'm sorry about what happened to him, Riley. I know you liked him. I'm sure the cops will figure it out."

"I'm sorry about what happened to him too," I said. "But I hardly knew him."

Ashleigh arched an eyebrow. "You two sure spent a lot of time together. I saw him waiting at your locker three times last week."

"You're keeping score?"

"Just noticing things, that's all."

Noticing them accurately. He had indeed waited for me three times in the past week. Each time he had greeted me with a shy hi.

"He wasn't a big talker," I told Ashleigh.

"But he asked you out, right?"

I shook my head. "He just wanted to talk. At least, that's all he ever did. He said he'd heard some things about me, like what happened this summer. Stuff from before I moved here too. I think he was just curious."

"You're saying he *didn't* ask you out?" Ashleigh looked disappointed for me.

"He didn't ask me out, and I'm fine with that."

"You didn't like him? You didn't like *Ethan Crawford*?"

"I liked him. He was okay, I guess."

"Okay? You guess?"

"But he never asked me out."

"But I heard—"

"You heard what?"

"I heard that he did."

"Where did you hear that?"

"In the girls' bathroom. I overheard some girls. One of them was Serena. The way she was trash-talking you—"

"She was trash-talking me? She doesn't even know me."

"From the way she was talking, I thought she'd caught you and Ethan together or something."

"Well, she didn't."

"Huh," Ashleigh said.

We stared across the street. Ashleigh sipped her latte. She was getting close to the bottom when I spotted Aunt Ginny in the police parking lot.

"I'll be right back," I said.

I caught Aunt Ginny as she was getting into her car.

"Did you find out who was on the roof?" I asked.

"Riley, I have work to do. I'm on my way to Ethan's house."

I didn't envy her that.

"There was someone else on the roof, Aunt Ginny. I told Detective Martin, but I don't think—"

"He told me what you said. We know what we're doing, Riley."

"So you're looking for that person?"

Aunt Ginny looked evenly at me. She unlocked her car and got in.

"Do you think he was pushed, Aunt Ginny?"

"Goodbye, Riley." She turned the key in the ignition, and I watched her pull away.

I rode home thinking about Ethan and Ethan's dad, whom I had never met, and hoping that both Ashleigh and I were wrong, that Ethan hadn't been pushed and hadn't jumped. That it was an accident because accidents, as unpredictable as they are, are easier to understand than intentional violence or self-destruction. I tried to focus on my homework, but Ashleigh barraged me with texts, asking if I had heard anything new. I told her what I always told her— Aunt Ginny never talked about a case under active investigation. Ashleigh fed me every scrap of intelligence, ridiculous or otherwise, that came her way. This consisted of the following:

Somebody (it wasn't clear who) had heard somebody (identity also not clear) say that she or he had heard that Ethan was going to make up with Serena.

Somebody (again, not clear who) had heard that Ethan had asked me out and I had turned him down.

Somebody had heard that Ethan had asked me out and I had accepted and I had boasted to everyone I knew.

Somebody had heard that Andes had asked Serena out and she had turned him down.

Somebody had heard exactly the opposite: that Serena had asked Andes out and he had turned her down.

Did I say *intelligence*? I meant idle gossip.

I was sprawled on my bed, staring at the ceiling, when I heard car tires crunch over the gravel driveway. Aunt Ginny was home. When I met her on the back porch, she was getting out of a police car.

"Your car *still* isn't fixed?" I asked.

She rolled her eyes. "Every time I ask that lunatic about it, he tells me it'll be one more day. It's been five days already." She had taken her car in for minor repairs, and the wait was putting her in a bad mood. At least, that's how she would have described it. I knew better. She was *hangry*—in a grouchy mood induced by low blood sugar. I knew how to deal with that.

"I made that meatloaf you like, and there's mashed potatoes. I could have it ready in five minutes, if you'd like a snack," I said.

"I'll take a quick shower." She unholstered her firearm, removed the bullets from it, carried them directly to the lock box where she kept them when she was at home, and padded upstairs to change. By the time she returned, scrubbed, shampooed and pajamaed, I had a plate of hot food waiting. She tucked in. I sat down with her.

"How did Ethan's father take it?" I asked.

"Not well, poor man." This through a mouthful of mashed potato and meatloaf. "Did you know Ethan's brother is a paraplegic?"

"No." Ethan hadn't mentioned it. Nor had anyone else.

"Apparently it was a football accident." Aunt Ginny looked around the kitchen like a dog sniffing out more treats. I took the hint and cut her another piece of meatloaf. "He took a bad tackle. I think he was even more broken up than the father when I told them about Ethan."

"What about the person on the roof?"

Aunt Ginny polished off the last bite of meatloaf and the last blob of potato and sat back in her chair. "Tell me exactly what you saw," she said. Translation: She hadn't found him. Or her.

I repeated what had happened in as much detail as I could recall.

"Could you tell if it was a man or a woman? Young or old?"

"The sun was directly behind the person's head. All I saw was a shape."

"Long hair, short hair?"

"Not long. At least, not long and loose. It could have been pulled back though." I knew how all this sounded—my description, such as it was, fit almost everyone.

"Did you find anything on the roof, Aunt Ginny? Did anyone at the rec center see someone go up there?"

"The security guard at the front desk left right after his shift finished at three thirty, before it happened. He got called out of town. His mother had a bad fall. He'll be back the day after tomorrow. I'll talk to him then."

"There was a swim meet going on. There were lots of people inside. Someone must have seen something."

"If anyone did, I haven't heard from him or her yet. I haven't even found anyone who saw Ethan go up to the roof in the first place. We're making an appeal to the public tomorrow. Maybe that will turn up something." She sighed. "It's been a long day. I'm going to bed."

THREE

My grandpa Jimmy, who mostly raised me, was a rock-and-roll musician from the old days. He'd had some big hits in the sixties, faded out during the seventies when disco music was big, made a brief comeback in the eighties, faded again in the nineties (faded from the airwaves, that is), but through it all kept right on touring. Jimmy had a lot of fans, and they had stayed loyal to him no matter what else was going on in the world of music. He had also made new fans everywhere he went because he put on a great show. Jimmy and his band had been together since forever, and Jimmy had an unshakable credo when it came to going onstage: he put on the best show he possibly could, because in every audience, he said, there might be someone who was seeing him for the first time, and Jimmy wanted that person to come back. There also might be someone seeing him for the last time, and Jimmy wanted to make sure they went away with something to remember.

Jimmy had loved to sing and play music. People who had seen his grizzled face, too-long hair and too-scruffy jeans and concluded that his brain was as wooly as the rest of him would have been mistaken. There was a lot to Jimmy that you'd never guess from a casual glance. For example, he had loved going to museums and art galleries. And because he'd toured not just in North America but around the world, and because I'd always gone with him, we'd gotten to see a lot of art.

There was one picture we'd both loved. It was in the Musée des Beaux-Arts in Paris. It was painted hundreds of years ago by a man named Pieter Brueghel. In the foreground of the painting, a man is plowing a field, while in the distance a ship sails by. Near the bottom right-hand corner of the painting, there are two legs sticking out of the water. They are the legs of a man who has plunged into the sea. I didn't notice them at first. Jimmy had to point them out. *That's Icarus*, he said. Icarus's father, Daedalus, was a slave in ancient Greece. He desperately wanted freedom, so he made wings out of feathers held together by wax for himself and his son. He warned Icarus not to fly too close to the sun, because its heat would melt the wax and destroy the wings. But Icarus didn't listen, so instead of gaining his freedom, he fell into the sea and drowned. But here's the real point of the painting. The people in the gallery looking at the painting see Icarus as he plummets to his death. But no one in the painting notices him. The ship sails on, its crew and passengers oblivious to the boy. The farmer plows his field without even a glance at the sea below. Chickens and dogs go about their business. Life goes on. Jimmy said that's what the painting was about. Life goes on, no matter what.

That's what it felt like the next day at school.

It wasn't that Ethan's death went unnoticed. It didn't. There was an announcement first thing that morning. But by then it was day-old news. There had been fifteen hours' worth of texts and calls back and forth among his friends and acquaintances. There had been tears, judging from the puffy eyes of a lot of girls the next morning. Serena showed up at school, which apparently stunned her friends. She didn't last long. She burst into tears in the middle of her first class of the day and didn't stop—couldn't stop, some people said—even after a friend took her to the office, where her parents were summoned to come and get her. The table in the cafeteria that was deemed property of the football team was quieter than usual. In fact, it was eerily quiet. But school went on. Teachers droned on. Kids took notes to stay awake.

Before the day was out, kids—even kids who'd known Ethan all their lives—had started acting more like they usually did, because they were still here even if Ethan wasn't, and they still had to get through the next class and then rush to their after-school jobs or meet their boyfriends or whatever. Even Ashleigh, who had spent the first half of lunch dissecting what she had observed or heard about Serena's behavior (*Uncontrollable crying? Her? She's in control, all the time. If you ask me…*), paused to give Charlie a hard time, the way she always did. Life goes on.

"I almost didn't recognize you," she said when he showed up, lunch bag in hand. "This is the first time in ages that I haven't had to reach for my sunglasses."

Charlie's response: "Huh?"

"Your jacket. You're not wearing it."

At the end of summer, Charlie and his mother had visited Charlie's aunt in Toronto. Charlie had come back with new clothes for school. His prized acquisition was a bright-yellow jacket. And by bright, I mean as bright as the sun overhead at noon. You could see Charlie coming from clear across town when he was wearing that jacket. Ashleigh had started in on him right away, and so far hadn't let up.

"It was time for a change," Charlie said. He dropped down in the chair next to mine and tossed his lunch bag onto the table. He didn't open it.

"I hope you didn't let Ashleigh's opinion stop you from wearing it," I said.

"Liar," Ashleigh declared. "You hope exactly the opposite. That jacket is so loud I actually hear it before I see it."

She wasn't the only person to tease Charlie about his jacket. Some people said he looked like a bumblebee. Or a giant canary. Some said he should be a crossing guard, because he was more visible than a set of traffic lights. Or that he could go hunting with absolutely no fear of being mistaken for a deer.

Mike Winters and his buddies, who used to call Charlie Lightbulb because his last name is Edison, now called him Yellow Light, like a traffic signal, and made jokes about him being slow.

Usually Charlie ignored all the comments—except for Ashleigh's. Usually he told her that she had no taste (to which she'd respond, *And you're color-blind*) or chided her for acting like a self-appointed fashion cop. Today he just slouched in his chair.

"It's okay, Charlie," I said quietly. "I'm not mad at you."

"Mad at him?" Ashleigh's antennae quivered at the possibility of juicy news. "Mad at him for what?"

"That's between Charlie and me." I looked at him. "How's your hand?"

Ashleigh's attention darted to Charlie. She waited for him to answer.

Charlie stood up and jammed his hands in the pockets of his jeans.

"I gotta go," he said.

"But you haven't touched your lunch."

"I'm not hungry."

"What's eating him?" Ashleigh asked as she watched him go. He hadn't even taken his lunch bag with him. "With Ethan out of the picture, you'd think he'd be happy." She snagged his lunch bag and pulled it toward her.

"That's an awful thing to say. Charlie would never be happy because someone died."

"I don't mean happy like he's going to dance in the streets or anything. I just mean, you know, relieved. Because now he doesn't have to worry about Ethan." She opened Charlie's lunch bag and let out a squeal. "Score!" She lifted a small container from the bag and opened it. Inside was a butter tart. "Charlie's mom makes the best butter tarts I've ever tasted. Want a bite?"

"No. And for the last time, there was nothing going on between Ethan and me."

"There must have been something for Charlie to get so upset. You saw what he did to his hand, didn't you?"

"Did he tell you how he hurt it?"

"Yeah." She bit into the tart. A beatific smile crossed her lips. "Oh, this is so good. If you want a bite, you'd better say so now."

"What did he say, Ashleigh?"

"He said he punched a wall."

"He told me he fell. He made it sound like an accident."

"That's not an injury from a fall, Riley. It's what happens when someone smashes his fist into something much harder."

"Like a wall," I said.

"That's one possibility." Ashleigh gave me a meaningful look.

"What do you mean by that?" I asked. "Do you think Charlie lied to you about how he hurt his hand?"

"He lied to one of us," Ashleigh said. "Maybe he lied to both of us. He looked kind of shifty when I asked him what happened, as if he didn't want to talk about it."

He'd done the same thing with me too.

"Ashleigh, you don't think Charlie and Ethan—" I broke off. What was the matter with me? What was I thinking? There was no way Charlie would hurt anyone.

"All I'm saying is that something is definitely bothering him. Even with Ethan out of the picture— and believe me when I tell you that no one wanted Ethan away from you more than Charlie did—something is still eating him."

"You know him better than I do, Ashleigh. Are you worried?"

"I don't know. You think I should be?"

We looked at each other and shook our heads in unison.

"He must have punched a wall," Ashleigh said. "Charlie isn't the kind of guy who punches people— especially not a person on the football team."

I wanted to agree with her. According to Ashleigh, Charlie had always been a kid other kids picked on, mostly because he was smaller than most guys his age. He was certainly smaller than Ethan. But then I thought back to the summer, when I had first met Charlie. Some guys had been giving him a hard time at a beach party. Charlie had handily disposed of one of them, flipping him onto his back in the sand with one neat move. He'd been so pleased with himself. He'd announced to everyone that he'd been taking martial arts. I had no idea how much he had improved. Or how much confidence he'd gained. It was possible he'd learned enough and had gotten confident enough to take on Ethan. And if that was the case, what else might he have done?

I like to be active. I ride my bike almost everywhere. I love to go hiking. If there's a lake or a pool around, I like to swim. Some girls, it turns out, don't like phys ed class because they get all sweaty and their hair gets ruined. I'm not one of those girls. I don't mind phys ed. The phys ed teacher in Moorebridge though—that was another story.

His name was Bob McGruder. Fortysomething and clean-shaven, with a military-style buzz cut, bulging biceps and impressive pecs under a tight white T-shirt. Mid-priced sneakers peeked out under his track pants. He had a bark like a drill sergeant's. He was also the football coach.

A shrill whistle cut the air, and action died on the soccer field.

"You!" Mr. McGruder thundered at me from the side of the field while I and twenty-one classmates waited to see whom he would point to with his short blunt finger. "Donovan!" Right. Me again. "Are you blind?"

Blind? Me?

"No, sir!" I shouted back.

"I beg to differ, Donovan. You missed that opening. Your lack of focus is hurting your team." I glanced at my teammates, who were scattered across the prickly brown grass and who were, for the most part, looking hot, winded and bored. "You're in this game to win, aren't you?"

"Well…" I was in it because, frankly, I had no choice.

"If you're not in it to win it, you have no business being on the field," Mr. McGruder bellowed.

Maybe if it had been my first encounter with Mr. McGruder, I would have shrugged off his comment. But it wasn't. He was picking on me. Looking for things to criticize. Inventing them, if he had to. Like when he barked at me in the very first class of the year that I'd better learn to put my heart and soul into running laps or he would make sure I got extra practice. This while the rest of the class jogged leisurely in bunches, chatting to each other. When I protested one of his calls in team sports, he handed me more laps and lectured me on how the referee was always right, no matter what. When I said that even referees make mistakes, as has been proved time and again by instant replays on television, he added yet more laps and wouldn't let me go to my next class until I finished. That got me into trouble with my English teacher, who was within sight of retirement and had no time for any book or poem written after the end of the Victorian era. I didn't have a problem with that. I like Dickens. Shakespeare too. Unlike my classmates, most of whom seemed bored out of their skulls.

You'd think I'd get used to the fact that every time I opened my mouth to Mr. McGruder, I ended up running more laps. A Labrador retriever could figure it out—if you don't want to get whacked on the nose with a rolled-up newspaper, don't bark. But the thing with bullies—and Mr. McGruder was bullying me for some reason—is that they never let up. Ever. So the choice wasn't shut up or run laps. The choice was stick up for myself or let him get away with bullying me again. The upside of sticking up for myself? (There's always an upside.) I was developing excellent cardiovascular capacity thanks to all the laps I ended up running.

Mr. McGruder stared at me and waited for my response, even though he hadn't actually asked a question.

"Just keep your mouth shut and play," Ashleigh hissed into my ear. "We have fifteen minutes until the bell rings. You don't want to do more laps, do you?"

I didn't.

But Mr. McGruder wouldn't let it go. "Did you hear me, Donovan?"

"Yes, sir! I'm either in it to win or I have no business being on the field."

"Please, please, please don't say anything else," Ashleigh said.

And I didn't. Not a word. Instead, I walked off the field.

"Where in the blue blazes do you think you're going?" Mr. McGruder roared.

"You said if I wasn't in it to win it…"

I heard Ashleigh groan behind me.

Mr. McGruder turned red in the face. "Get back to your position, *now*!"

"But you said—"

"Of course you're in it to win. That's what sport is all about. Play hard. Play to win."

"That's not what it's about to me," I said.

"Some people never learn," Ashleigh said in a voice just loud enough for me to hear.

"Get back to your position or I'll give you a detention," Mr. McGruder said.

"Detain away." I actually said that. "But everyone out here heard what you said. Unless I'm in it to win, I don't belong on the field. And since I'm not in it to win—"

He blew his whistle so long and so hard that the sound was still ricocheting around inside my head a full sixty seconds later. "I don't like your attitude, Donovan. I haven't liked it since day one. To the office, now." And in case I had lost my sense of direction along with my spirit of competition, he pointed the way.

I was happy to march off the field and take a place on the bench in the office. Ms. O'Shea, one of the school administrative assistants, held out her hand. I looked blankly at it.

"You were sent here?" she asked.

I nodded.

"I'll need the explanation slip," she said.

"I don't have one."

She sighed. "Who sent you?"

"Mr. McGruder."

"Ah." Apparently this changed things. She lowered her hand. "Your crime?"

I told her.

"Take a seat. Mr. Chen will see you when he's free."

A few minutes later a door behind the counter opened, and Ms. O'Shea waved me into the vice-principal's office.

"Mr. McGruder sent her," she said.

Mr. Chen looked at my empty hands. "No slip, huh?"

"No, sir."

"You want to tell me what happened?"

I gave him a rundown. I tried to be objective, as if I was reporting on the incident instead of having been the aggrieved party. I'm not sure how well I succeeded.

"Mr. McGruder gave me a choice," I said by way of conclusion. "Everyone out there heard him. You can't give someone a choice and then punish them when they don't make the one you want. That's not fair."

Mr. Chen surprised me by saying, "No, it's not." He leaned back in his chair. "Mr. McGruder was a professional athlete. Football. CFL. He's serious about his sport. He played two seasons before a knee injury benched him permanently. He started coaching after that, and it's thanks to him that we have the best

football team in our division. We've won the provincials half a dozen times in the past ten years, and we've
made the national semifinals twice. He knows how to
motivate players and get the best performance out of
them. That does, however, carry with it a certain...
enthusiasm for competition that may not be everyone's cup of tea."

"I'm not a football player, sir," I said. "And it was
just a PE class."

"I understand that, Riley. In fact—"

The door to Mr. Chen's office flew open, struck
the wall with a solid whack, bounced back and would
have slammed shut again had Mr. McGruder not
stopped it with one hand. He stormed in, his face set
in fury.

Mr. Chen regarded him calmly. "Bob," he said.
"I've been expecting you. Riley, wait outside while I
have a word with Mr. McGruder."

Gladly. I didn't want to be in the same room
with the man. I reclaimed my spot on the bench and
listened, along with everyone else in the office, to
Mr. McGruder's rant, which Mr. Chen's door did little
to muffle, let alone mute. He denounced my lack of
spirit and complained that it was undermining him

and giving the other girls a reason to slack off, and what was the matter with girls anyway, some of them looked like skeletons and none of them wanted to break a sweat, you had to threaten them with laps to get them to do anything. Ms. O'Shea glanced at me. One of my fellow benchees, a slouching girl, stared openly at me and refused to stop, even when I gave her a pointed *What's your problem?* look. She snickered in response.

Mr. Chen's door opened again, violently, and Mr. McGruder erupted from the small office like a lava plug from a volcano. He scowled at me as he swept past. Mr. Chen crooked a finger at me.

"I believe we've come to a compromise," he said when we were back in his office.

"But I didn't do anything wrong."

"I'm not saying you did. But I need to keep the peace around here, and Mr. McGruder feels strongly that the competitive spirit is a key component of an athletic education."

"In other words, either I cave in to his idea of sport or I'm doomed to run laps for the rest of my high school career?"

"Not at all. I said compromise, and I do mean compromise. I'm confident that once you and Coach get to know each other, all will be well. Now, due to an unfortunate illness, Coach's assistant has been sidelined temporarily. I have suggested—and Coach has agreed to—a replacement. You. Coach will have the opportunity to teach you about the competitive spirit. And you will have the opportunity to air your point of view."

"Or you could just tell him to leave me alone unless I actually do something wrong." It was hardly a bold suggestion, but Mr. Chen rejected it outright.

"You show up for two weeks, and then it's over. Think of it as an exercise in understanding the other person's point of view. That's often the first step in the peaceful resolution of any dispute. And you never know, you might actually learn something. Apparently we have a shot at the finals again this year." Mr. Chen paused. "At least, we did before Ethan—" He broke off. "The prevailing feeling among the team members is that they should give it their all and make it to the finals as a tribute to Ethan. Maybe you could help lift team spirit."

I could have argued. This exercise in mutual understanding sounded like punishment to me, and I had done nothing wrong. But I didn't want to be picked on for the rest of the year either.

"Do you think it will make a difference? He'll leave me alone?"

"If it doesn't, you come to me and I'll deal with it."

"Football is that important, huh?"

Mr. Chen shrugged. "I don't understand it either, but yes, around here it is. Report to practice after last period."

FOUR

"That's not fair," Charlie declared later that day. "You should complain to Mrs. Dekes." Mrs. Dekes is our school principal. She is also my English teacher's sister.

"You're just jealous because Riley's going to be around all those totally ripped athletes," Ashleigh said.

"I am not." Tellingly, Charlie's face turned red. "You're missing the point. Riley didn't do anything. What right does Mr. Chen have to punish her by turning her into a gofer for Coach McGruder?"

"So you don't mind if she hangs around with the football team?"

"That has nothing to do with it." Charlie was sticking to his story.

I slammed my locker door. "I just want to get this over with as smoothly as possible. So I gotta go. If I'm even one second late, Mr. McGruder will probably make me do laps with the team."

I shouldered my backpack and hurried out to the athletics field. I needn't have worried about being late. Nothing was happening. The team had assembled in full football gear, but they were standing around watching Coach, who was locked in what seemed to be a dispute with Detective Martin while Aunt Ginny looked on.

"They're not going anywhere," Coach said to Detective Martin. "They'll all be right here in two hours' time. I won't let them leave. Come back then and talk to them."

"Sorry, Coach," Detective Martin said. "This is a death investigation. The sooner we finish our questioning, the sooner we can wrap it up and the sooner Ethan's family can get the answers they're looking for."

"This is a scheduled practice. Ethan would have wanted it to go on. Right, fellas?" Mr. McGruder looked at the players, who mumbled and nodded.

"We'll be as quick as we can," Detective Martin said, "but we have to be thorough." As he stepped away from Mr. McGruder, he spotted me, but he didn't say anything.

Mr. McGruder saw me too.

"It's about time," he said.

"I'm right on time." I checked my watch. I was.

"On time around here is five minutes early."

What a grouch! I looked pointedly at the team. They had lined themselves up loosely along the outer edges of the field, ready for questioning. In their bulky football gear, most of them dwarfed Aunt Ginny. She was working her way down the line, sorting them out, telling some to stand to one side and dismissing others back to Coach.

"Terrific," he muttered. "She's sending me all the rookies."

"The cops only want to speak to the guys who knew Crawford," one of the braver newbies said. The only thing most of them knew about Ethan was his reputation. Mr. McGruder cleared his throat noisily, consulted his clipboard and started them on laps while he waited for the detectives to finish with his starting lineup.

The rookies ran through a stringent series of calisthenics—jumping jacks, burpees, crunches and push-ups—and finished with a brisk relay through old tires to hone agility. By the time they had finished, all but three team members had joined in, and Mr. McGruder reluctantly started a full practice, grousing that he didn't really see the point because his star players were still tied up with the cops when they should have been "giving it their all for Crawford and making this team a winner."

Ten minutes before the end of practice, the three remaining players, including Andes, reported to Coach, who, for his part, shot an evil eye at Aunt Ginny, who had questioned the fullback at length. The look didn't surprise me. Coach struck me as just the kind of guy to have a negative attitude about female police officers. Aunt Ginny was used to that though. Her only response to Coach's glare was to glance at me, a quizzical expression on her face.

Coach finally dismissed the team and sent me to load the practice tires onto the cart that was used to transport them while he talked to the three players who had missed practice.

As I trotted over to the tire obstacle course, I heard him ask, "What did they want?" I slowed down, hoping to hear the answer, but Coach noticed and saw me look back over my shoulder. "What are you waiting for, Donovan? Get a move on. Those tires aren't going to roll themselves back to the equipment locker."

I got a move on. The tires weren't so much heavy—maybe twenty pounds each—as they were awkward and bulky. And there were a lot of them to get onto a small cart, which meant I had to stack them carefully. That became more and more difficult the higher the stacks became. I was struggling with them when Coach dismissed the remaining three players. He checked my progress, shook his head in disgust and dispatched one of the players to me.

"Coach says you need a hand," he said. He was massive—a good head and shoulders taller than me and twice as wide even without all his padding.

"I'm Riley," I said.

"Yeah. I heard. Munster." He grabbed a tire and flung it expertly onto the top of one of the piles.

"Huh?"

"Munster. That's my name." He swung another tire into place. "Well, really it's Matt. Matt Mason. But everyone calls me Munster, you know, on account of that old TV show and how big I am."

"Kind of like Andes, right?" I said.

He nodded, flipped the last few tires effortlessly onto the cart and positioned himself to push the cart across the field to the school.

"You want to grab the front and steer?" he said.

"Sure." I threw my backpack onto the top of the pile and grabbed the front of the cart. Munster pushed and the cart jerked forward, almost knocking me over.

"So," I shouted back over my shoulder, "what did the cops want?"

"They had a bunch of questions about Crawford. You knew him, right?"

"Sort of." I had to trot to keep ahead of the cart and steer it toward the school. "What did they say? Do they know what happened?"

"If they did, they didn't say. You know cops. They never say."

I wondered what kind of experience had taught him that.

"You want my opinion? I don't think they think it was an accident."

"What makes you say that?"

"They asked a million questions, that lady cop especially. She's like a pit bull. She kept asking the same things over and over. *Guys from the team hang out up there, right? Are some guys there more than others? Did Crawford go up there a lot? Were you up there that day? What time were you there? When did you leave? Did you see anyone else up there? Was anyone else up there when you left—besides Crawford?*"

"What time *were* you up there?"

Munster grinned. "It's true what they say about you, huh?"

"What do you mean?"

"You're nosy."

There was no point in denying it. "You were up there, right?"

"Yeah. At lunchtime. That lady cop grilled me about it. *Did you have any beefs with Crawford? Did anyone else? What kind of beefs? Did they work it out? How did they work it out? Did anyone ever threaten anyone else?* On and on." He looked evenly at me.

"I didn't have anything to do with what happened to Ethan, and I don't know who did."

We reached the rear entrance to the school basement. I opened the door and jumped aside to allow Munster to shove the cart through. I followed him as he maneuvered it around a tight corner and down a long hallway.

"Done." He straightened up and stretched. "Time to hit the shower."

"What did you say?" I asked.

"I said it's time to hit the shower."

"No, I mean to the cops."

He eyed me with amusement. "What's it to you? Is all that talk about you and Ethan true? I heard he started hanging out with you after he dumped Serena. Who started it, him or you?"

"Nobody started anything. He just showed up at my locker one day and introduced himself."

"He had his eye on you from the first day of school."

"He did?" That was news to me.

Munster looked me over from head to toe. "I guess I can see why. Did you two get all hot and heavy?"

"No!" I felt my cheeks burning. "For your information, nothing happened. I didn't even know he'd broken up with Serena at first." I didn't find out until after she'd given me the evil eye a couple of times, and then it was Ashleigh who had enlightened me. "He just wanted to talk, that's all." And most of that talk had been about me—stuff he'd heard about me, questions about the different things I'd gotten mixed up in, questions about Aunt Ginny.

"That's Crawford. A real talker." He turned to go.

"Matt?"

"Munster," he said. "Everyone calls me Munster." He seemed proud of the name.

"Okay, Munster. What *did* you tell them?"

"The cops?" He grinned again. "Let's just say I answered all their questions." He waved his hand in a goodbye salute and loped down the corridor and out of sight.

I scrambled up onto the cart to retrieve my backpack and went back outside to find my bike. That's when Ashleigh texted me. **Where r u? Come here now.**

Where r u? I texted back.

Police station.

I jumped on my bike and found Ashleigh minutes later on the sidewalk in front of the police station. She wasn't alone. A small crowd had gathered. Everyone was looking at the same scene.

FIVE

Three people stood outside the police station—Aunt Ginny, Josh Martin and a tall, thin man in a gray overcoat. I'd never seen him before. Ashleigh told me he was Ethan's dad. He was the one doing the talking. He stabbed the air with his index finger while he spoke. The finger was pointed at Aunt Ginny.

Aunt Ginny's face was unreadable. It was the face she showed to co-workers, citizens and wrongdoers. It was the impartial, ever-vigilant, ever-cautiously-suspicious face that Aunt Ginny seemed to think was needed in her job. Sometimes I wondered what people would think if they saw her the way I did when she was at home and safely out of the public eye. She slouched around in her pajamas, eating ice cream out of the container with a soup spoon when she was angry or frustrated. She sulked, silent and withdrawn, when she'd been assigned to a small case instead of a major crime. She kicked the furniture after most encounters with the chief of police, who stuck like a burr to the concept of chain of command, which meant that he generally addressed himself to Detective Martin, even when Aunt Ginny was right there with them.

Now Detective Martin held up a hand in a calming gesture. Ethan's dad turned to him. His face was flushed. But he stopped stabbing his finger at Aunt Ginny and listened to what the detective was saying. The two exchanged more words before Detective Martin put his hand on Mr. Crawford's shoulder and walked him to his car. Aunt Ginny watched them. I couldn't even begin to guess what she was thinking.

"What do you think that was all about?" Ashleigh asked.

I wished I knew.

I headed home to start dinner. While the chicken baked, I watched the local news. Ethan Crawford's death was the lead story.

"Dr. Timothy Crawford, father of the dead boy, has accused one of the detectives in charge of the death investigation of incompetence," said a perky brunette news reader with impossibly aqua eyes. Dr. Crawford appeared on the screen.

"My son has died tragically," he said. His face was gray and lined with grief, but his voice was sharp with outrage. "We—his brother and I—want to lay him to rest next to his mother. We want to mourn him. But Detective Virginia McFee is insisting that there is more to his death than a tragic accident. She is spreading lies about my son and suggesting things about him that are untrue. I have spoken to the chief of police. I have demanded that he take the matter in hand."

Spreading lies? Aunt Ginny?

Cut to the chief of police, a portly, gray-haired man who had lived and policed in the region for his whole life. "When a young person dies—when any person in our community dies—suddenly and unexpectedly, our duty is to conduct a thorough investigation of the circumstances. We are doing exactly that in the Ethan Crawford case, and Dr. Crawford has my assurance that we will wrap this up quickly so that the family can find closure."

His statement was vague. He didn't mention Aunt Ginny. Had he reprimanded her? Had he removed her from the case?

It was nearly an hour before I had a chance to find out. I waited until Aunt Ginny had hung her jacket on the back of a kitchen chair and was digging into the plate of food I'd placed in front of her.

"You're going to get indigestion if you don't slow down," I said as she shoveled chicken into her mouth.

"I have to get back to work," she said. With her mouth full.

"Because of what the chief said?"

Her fork, on a return trip to her plate to load up again, hovered in midair.

"He was on TV. On the news," I said.

"Oh. What did he say?"

"That the investigation into Ethan's death is going to be wrapped up quickly."

Aunt Ginny shook her head angrily. "They hire you to do a job, and then they won't let you do it."

"What do you mean?"

No answer.

"Ethan's dad was on TV. He said you were spreading lies about Ethan."

"Did he?"

"Why would he say that, Aunt Ginny?"

No answer.

"Are you still part of the investigation, Aunt Ginny? Or did—"

"I don't even know why Dr. Crawford is so upset. He demanded—and I do mean demanded; the man likes to be in charge—an update on the investigation, and I gave him one. I told him we haven't ruled anything out yet, and that includes suicide. For some reason, that enraged him. His son is dead. You'd think he'd want to know what happened. Instead, he's acting like he can't wait to get him in the ground. And then Josh told him that he's going to handle the case personally." So that was what had been going on in the parking lot. "I'm still on the case, but I'm not supposed to do anything without Josh's permission. He's in charge."

Aunt Ginny liked to be in the thick of things. She'd thought when she got hired that she would be handling important investigations. She is a detective, after all. She hadn't counted on how much her job would be influenced by local politics and a web of local relationships in which she was regarded as an outsider. It all drove her crazy, and she wasn't a patient person to begin with. I steered the conversation away from the chief.

"You don't really think it was suicide, do you?"

"I never said it was. I said it hadn't been ruled out. And it hasn't." She eyed me speculatively. "How well did you know this boy, Riley?"

"I didn't. Not really. He is—was—a year ahead of me."

"Did you ever speak to him?"

"A couple of times. But he didn't talk much about himself."

"What about other kids? What do they say about him?"

"Haven't you interviewed his friends, Aunt Ginny?"

"A few of them. Before Josh took over. I've been trying to get hold of his girlfriend—"

"Serena Dobbs."

Aunt Ginny perked up. "You know her?"

"I know who she is, but don't get excited. She's the kind of person *everyone* knows, but only a select number of people are actually admitted to her inner circle."

"Sounds just like your mother," Aunt Ginny said.

"Really?" My mom had died when I was a baby.

"But in a nice way," she added hastily. "I used to envy how easily she made friends." She banished the past with a shake of her head. "So I take it you're not part of Serena's inner circle."

"Not even close. But you know where she lives, right?"

"Her parents are protective to the point of obstructive. From what I've been able to gather, Serena broke up with Ethan. Part of the problem that led to the breakup was Ethan's behavior. Everyone we spoke to told us he'd changed in the week or so before he died. He had something on his mind, but he never talked about it. The next thing you know, he's found dead after falling from a rooftop terrace surrounded by a four-foot-high steel railing with plexiglass inserts bolted to it, making it demonstrably impossible for his fall to have been the result of an accident—"

"So you're saying he had to have jumped on purpose."

"We haven't ruled it out. We haven't ruled anything out."

"Except accident."

"Except accident involving only Ethan."

She had my full attention.

"But it still could have been an accident—is that what you're saying? Like, say, if he was fooling around with someone up there or something like that?" I tried to picture how that would have worked. "Maybe that's why whoever was up there with Ethan hasn't come forward yet." I glanced at my aunt. "No one has, have they?"

She shook her head.

"Maybe they're afraid to. Maybe it really was an accident, and they're afraid they're going to get blamed for what happened."

"Not coming forward isn't helping whoever you saw—assuming there really was someone up there. It raises a lot of questions."

"Do you think someone pushed Ethan?"

She looked evenly at me. "As I told Dr. Crawford, we haven't ruled out anything yet. And we won't be able to until we complete our investigation."

"Do you think Serena knows something?" I asked.

"I would have to interview her before I could answer that question." She stood up. "I have to get back to work."

"I talked to one of the guys on the football team. You and Josh spoke to him too. He was on the roof that day."

"Everyone was on the roof that day."

"*Everyone?*"

"Let's just say there was more than one person up there that day, although apparently not at the time Ethan fell. At least, that's what we've been told."

"You think someone is lying?"

She slipped on her jacket and ignored my question. "What were you doing at football practice anyway?"

"I'm helping Coach McGruder for a few days."

"Good god, why? I swear that man is the biggest Neanderthal on the planet."

"You know Coach?" I asked. She'd never mentioned him.

She stiffened. "It's a long story." She zipped her jacket. "I'll probably be late. Don't wait up for me."

By the next day, everyone seemed to have slipped back into their normal routines. If anyone noticed an Ethan-Crawford-shaped hole in the fabric of the school, no one mentioned it. Charlie seemed more or less back to his regular self and was still indignant about the agreement I'd made with Mr. Chen.

"If it gets Coach off my back, it's worth it. And who knows, I might learn something."

"About football? It's about time," Ashleigh said. She was a staunch supporter of the school team and therefore critical of my almost complete lack of knowledge of the sport.

"About Ethan," I said.

"What do you mean?" Charlie asked.

"Someone was on the rec-center roof when Ethan fell." Or was pushed, accidentally or on purpose. Or jumped. "Maybe someone on the team knows something. Maybe I'll hear something."

"Why are you getting involved in it?" Charlie said. "Why don't you leave it to the cops?"

"I want to help if I can. What's wrong with that?"

"You want to help because of how you felt about Ethan."

What was wrong with him? "I want to help because someone I knew—and you knew—is dead."

"Riley." Ashleigh touched my arm.

Charlie glowered at me and stalked away. Clearly, I was wrong about him. He wasn't back to normal. Something was bothering him. Something to do with Ethan.

Baseball had been Jimmy's game. He used to listen to it on the radio late at night when he was a kid, tuning to any station he could find that was broadcasting a game. Apart from local league games, which he'd loved to watch in whatever town he was playing, radio was the only way Jimmy followed baseball. I don't know if he ever sat in the stands at a major league game. I know I never saw him watch one on television.

But on countless summer and fall nights when he didn't have a gig, he'd lean back in his seat on the bus or prop himself up against pillows in bed and listen, a faraway look in his eyes as he visualized the plays the announcer was describing.

So I guess it's no surprise that baseball was also my game. I could bat okay. I was a great catcher. And boy, when I played pickup games with the band and the crew, I was a champion base stealer. At least, I used to think I was. Now, when I look back, I can't help thinking the guys had let me rob them blind. I was a little kid and the only female among a busload of guys, some of them missing their own kids back home. One thing was for sure though: I never watched football. I didn't even have a firm grasp of the rules. That made football practice boring for me. Or it would have if it hadn't been for Coach.

"You're late, Donovan" was the first thing he said to me.

I checked my watch. By real-world standards I was four minutes early. In Coach's world I was one minute late. I didn't bother to argue.

"Tires." Coach nodded at the cart that sat at the edge of the field.

"I'm going to need help," I said.

Coach scowled. "For the love of…" He blew his whistle and shouted something that sounded like "Tonka." This turned out to be a football player as massive as Andes and Munster. "Get that cart over to the other side of the field so this little lady can set up," Coach ordered him.

Without breaking stride, Tonka jogged to the cart, braced his hands against the back of it and pushed it effortlessly across the grassy field. He resumed his place on the field, leaving me to scramble to the top of the heap and start throwing down tires. I was dragging the last one into place when the team descended on me to run the course.

The guys in the front—the starting lineup—had no problem. I think they could have run that course blindfolded. The rookies were another story. A few of them miscalculated where to put their feet and landed on the sides of tires. Most of them caught themselves before they fell. One big guy with more fat than muscle on him crashed to the ground. From the howl of derision that went up, I gathered it wasn't his first time. Coach ordered him to the back of the line to try again.

You know how some people can take a good ribbing and not let it faze them? Well, the rookie wasn't one of those people. Coach had him in his sights for the rest of practice, yelling at him—*Faster! Slower! Pattern, pattern, pattern!*—rattling the poor guy. Every time he made a mistake, which was roughly every time he attempted a practice move, Coach blew his whistle and called him an idiot or a klutz or asked him how long he thought he'd last with the team if he kept up the way he was going. The other rookies looked both terrified and grateful at the same time—terrified that they would make a fatal mistake and be subjected to the same treatment as their poor teammate, and grateful that their colleague was sucking up all of Coach's attention so that the odd time one or other of them messed up, Coach didn't notice.

The guys on the starting lineup were as bad as Coach. They hooted and hollered every time the rookie made a mistake. Then I heard Munster say, "Coach has it in for that guy the way he had it in for Crawford."

I knew what it felt like to be picked on by Coach. So had Ethan, by the sound of it. I waited for Munster to say something else, but he was distracted by the sudden appearance of Serena on the sidelines. Munster nudged Andes, who broke from the field and jogged over to her. Coach's whistle cut the air in protest.

"Sorry, Coach," Andes called back over his shoulder. "I just need a minute." To Serena, he said, "Are you okay?"

Maybe she said she was, and maybe she wasn't. I couldn't tell. She didn't stop to talk to Andes. She breezed past him and came straight at me.

"Why?" she demanded. "Why was he spending so much time with you?"

"Serena." I had to back up because she'd come so close to me. Too close. I could smell her minty-fresh toothpaste. "Hi."

"Why?" she said. "Why you? What did you do to him?"

What did *I* do? "I don't know what you're talking about."

"He kept ditching me to go off and do something, but he never told me what, not even when I asked him. Then I started seeing him with you."

"He talked to me a couple of times, that's all."

"A couple of times? More like a couple of times a day!"

"That's not true."

"What about his phone? Why did he get a new phone?"

"What?" What was she talking about?

"They found a cell phone on the roof. The SIM card was missing. They say it was Ethan's phone. It had his fingerprints on it. But his father found his phone at home. He hadn't turned it on in days. Why? Why did he need another phone? What did you two talk about?"

We two?

"Serena, I never talked to him on the phone. We never texted either."

"He must have said something."

"About what?"

"About me."

"I'm sorry. He didn't."

Tears welled up in her eyes.

"He just asked me a bunch of stuff about me and my aunt, that's all. He wasn't interested in me," I said.

"Right. He ditches me to hang out with you, but he's not interested in you."

"Honestly, he wasn't." At least, he never said he was.

She stared at me. Her voice was quieter when she asked, "Did he seem depressed?"

"He was quiet. But I don't know what he was usually like."

"Something was bothering him. He was upset. I know he was. But he would never talk about it." Tears dribbled down her cheek. "Was it me?"

"I don't know."

"But he spent so much time with you."

"We talked three or four times, that's all."

Her face hardened again. "You're lying."

"I'm not, I swear."

Andes appeared behind her and slipped an arm around her shoulders. She flinched and spun around, furious. When she saw who it was, she relaxed.

"Is everything okay?" Andes asked.

"I don't understand." She wiped her tears, but they kept flowing. "I don't understand what's going on. They're saying it wasn't an accident. What does that mean? If it wasn't an accident, what happened? What was going on with him? He usually told me everything, but all of a sudden he got so quiet and withdrawn. I should have known something was wrong. I should have done something."

Andes held her while she cried. "Coach was giving him a hard time," he said. "He was off his game."

Serena pulled away just far enough so that she could look up at him. "See? I should have noticed that, but I didn't. And he didn't tell me. I should have known. I should have done something."

Coach's whistle shrilled again.

Andes squeezed Serena's shoulder. Serena smiled wanly at him and watched as he trotted off to join the others on the field. She turned back to me. I didn't know what to say. I needn't have worried. She left without a word. I thought about what she had said. Ethan had been quieter than usual before he died. He'd apparently had something on his mind. But what? Did it have something to do with why he had died? And what about his sudden interest in me? What had that been about?

Practice was over, the tires had been transported back to their resting spot with the help of Munster (*thank you, Munster*), and I was back on the field, heading for my bike, when I spotted someone on the roof of the rec center. Detective Martin. I watched his head appear and disappear over the railing above me. If he noticed me, he didn't say anything. He was too focused on what he was doing. By the time I was unlocking my bike, he was back at ground level, walking across the parking lot with Aunt Ginny. They stopped not far from where I was standing. I ducked down behind the nearest car so that I could hear what they were saying.

"Any luck?" Detective Martin asked Aunt Ginny.

"The guard is back in town, so I'm heading over to talk to him," she said. "I spoke to the administrator. She says she sees kids going up and down the stairwell all the time. Not just kids from the football team either. All kinds of kids are in and out of that place every day of the week. And the day Ethan died, there was a regional swim meet. There were busloads of kids in there. Still, she's agreed to come to the station as soon as her shift is over to look at pictures and see if anything jogs her memory. You?"

"Nothing much. You stick with the guard and the administrator. I have a few things to chase down."

"Like what?"

"Just do your job, McFee, and I'll do mine."

I heard footsteps coming toward me and dove behind the car like a criminal. Nothing happened. No one called my name. No one said, "Aha!" When I finally came up for air, both Detective Martin and Aunt Ginny were gone.

SIX

The police car showed up at seven o'clock, driven by the police officer who had been first on the scene the day that Ethan fell.

"Detective Martin wants to talk to you," he said.

I knew that already. He had called and asked me to come in.

We want to talk to you about Ethan Crawford, he had told me. *I'm sending a car.*

I was surprised Aunt Ginny wasn't the one to call me. She had told me that Josh Martin was in charge of the case now, but it still puzzled me when I was ushered into an interview room where Detective Martin was waiting for me—alone.

"Have a seat, Riley," he said.

I sat. Where was Aunt Ginny?

"I asked you to come in because I need to ask you some questions about Ethan Crawford. You're not under arrest, nor are you a suspect at this time. Do you understand?"

Wait a minute! "Suspect? Suspect in what?"

"Do you understand, Riley?"

"Yes. But—"

"You are under no obligation to answer my questions, but I'm sure you want to help us get to the bottom of what happened to Ethan. I have to caution you, however, that if you do answer my questions, anything you say can be used against you in subsequent proceedings. Do you understand?"

Subsequent proceedings? What was going on?

"Do you understand, Riley?"

"I thought you said I wasn't a suspect."

"You're not."

"Then why are you talking about subsequent proceedings?"

The question seemed to annoy him.

"It's procedure. I have to give you this caution. Now do you understand or not?"

"I understand, but—"

"Furthermore, as a juvenile, you are entitled to have a parent, guardian or some other adult present when you answer my questions. Do you understand?"

I did. "My aunt Ginny…"

"Do you want me to call her in? You have the right to have her here. However, you should be aware that if you ask her to come in here as your guardian, she will have to be removed from this case. It would be a conflict of interest for an investigating officer to attend this interview as your guardian. As a police officer, her job is to determine the truth of this case. As your guardian, she has a duty to protect you and your interests. The two don't necessarily coincide."

I looked right at him, but his face was like a rigid plastic mask. It was impossible to make out what was going on behind it.

He had said I wasn't a suspect. He'd read it from the paper he had in front of him. I hadn't done anything wrong. I wasn't even sure what was going on. Did Detective Martin's caution mean that the police had reached a conclusion about Ethan's death? Did the fact that I wasn't a suspect mean that suspects were being sought and, therefore they had concluded that someone had been involved in Ethan's death? Detective Martin's questions would give me a good idea what he was thinking. As for dragging Aunt Ginny into this, there was one thing I knew for a fact. If Aunt Ginny was pulled off the case—especially if it turned out to be a homicide case—on my account, there would be no living with her.

"I don't need anyone with me," I said.

"You're declining your right to have an adult present?"

"Yes."

He shoved a paper across the table. "Please read this aloud and initial that you understand what you're signing."

The paper outlined what he had already told me. After I'd initialed every clause, I signed at the bottom. He took the paper from me and tucked it into a file folder. He set that aside and pulled something out of his pocket. He slid it across the table to me. It was in a plastic baggie.

"Do you recognize this?"

"It's mine." The look of satisfaction in his eyes told me he already knew that. The item in the baggie was the green-and-gold four-leaf-clover charm that Charlie had given me, the one I'd attached to the loop on my backpack. "I've been looking for it. I lost it."

"Lost it? When?"

"I don't know exactly. But I noticed it missing after school the day before yesterday."

"The day Ethan Crawford fell from the roof of the rec center?"

"Yes. Where did you find it?"

That's when it struck me. I had last seen Detective Martin on the roof of the rec center.

"Would it surprise you to learn that I found that"—he nodded at the charm—"on the rec-center roof?"

I stared at it. How had it gotten up there?

"Do you want to tell me what it was doing up there, Riley?"

"I don't know." I leaned forward for a closer look. The little clasp didn't look damaged, and I knew for a fact that the loop on my backpack was in perfect condition. I had checked. So how had the charm fallen off? And how had it ended up on the roof?

"Were you on the roof that day, Riley?"

"No."

"Are you sure?"

"Yes. I'm positive."

"And you have no idea how your charm ended up there?" His face was dead serious now. He was scaring me.

"Maybe Ethan found it after I lost it. Maybe he picked it up and was going to give it back to me." It was possible. But I had no idea if Ethan was the kind of guy who would notice a charm on a girl's backpack.

"That wasn't found on Ethan. It was found on the roof." He sat forward in his chair. "Here's how I understand the sequence of events, Riley. You told us you were walking across the athletic field on your way to where you had left your bicycle. You said you heard someone scream and that you went to investigate, which is when you saw Ethan lying on the ground. The girls who saw him first didn't actually see him fall. He was already on the ground. But the one who was the first to see him there turned to look because she said she heard something hit the ground."

Like a sack of sand. I cringed when I remembered the cheerleader's words.

"Classes ended that day at three twenty. The cheerleaders got to the area behind the rec center to begin their practice at three forty-five. That means there were twenty-five minutes between the time classes ended and the time Ethan went off that roof." He leaned forward across the table. "What did you do after school ended that day, Riley?"

"I went to my locker to get my things."

"You went directly to your locker?"

"Yes. Then I waited for my friend."

He asked for the name of the friend.

"How long did you wait for her?" he asked.

"Five minutes."

"Five minutes? Are you sure?"

"She was late. I looked at the clock."

"And then?"

"We talked, and then she had to go. She had something to do. I went to the rec center to get my bike."

"And then?"

"I heard one of the cheerleaders scream."

He sat back and stared at me.

"So if I were to talk to your friend Ashleigh, she would confirm that you and she spoke for approximately fifteen or twenty minutes before you two parted company?"

That didn't sound right. "It was more like a couple of minutes."

"So five minutes waiting for your friend and a couple of minutes talking to her. That takes us to three thirty at the latest. What did you do between three thirty and three forty-five, when Ethan was found? And how did that"—he jabbed at the charm inside the baggie—"get on the roof?"

"I don't know how it got there. I told you. I'd lost it. I was looking for it."

"Did you go up to the roof to look?"

"No!" Maybe I said it too loudly. Maybe I sounded too insistent. Detective Martin leaned forward again and stared at me as if he thought he could read my thoughts. "I looked for it in the schoolyard," I said. "I thought maybe it had fallen off my backpack, so on my way to the bike lockup, I looked for it. That's what I did after I left Ashleigh."

"Did you see anyone else outside the school at that time? Anyone who might have seen you?"

I tried to think. I didn't remember seeing anyone, but that didn't mean there wasn't someone out there who might have seen me.

"I don't know."

"You don't know if you saw anyone?"

"I was looking at the ground the whole time."

"Nobody called to you—a friend, a classmate?"

I shook my head. "I was looking for that charm when I heard a scream."

"You're sure you weren't up on the roof?"

"I'm positive. I didn't even see Ethan that day. Not until after." After he'd hit the ground.

Detective Martin let silence fill the room. He seemed to wait forever before settling back in his chair and saying, "Tell me about the last time you saw Ethan. When was that?"

"Saturday. He texted me. We met up at the park."

"Because he texted you?"

"Yes. He said he wanted to ask me something."

"About what?"

"He never said. He seemed, I don't know, distracted." Half the time I'd been sure he wasn't even listening to me. I couldn't figure out why he'd wanted to see me when clearly he had something else on his mind.

Had he been thinking about whatever led to his fall from the roof?

"Did he say anything? Do you know what he was distracted about?" Detective Martin prodded.

Had I missed something in Ethan? What if he'd wanted to tell to me what was bothering him but had difficulty finding the words? If I'd forced him to talk, could I have prevented his death?

"You said I didn't have to answer any questions if I didn't want to," I said. "It says the same thing on that paper I signed. Well, I don't want to answer any more. Not until you tell me what happened to Ethan."

"You knew him. As I understand it, he broke up with his girlfriend so that he could be with you."

"That's not true." Who had told him that? Serena? "What happened to Ethan? Did someone kill him? Or are you saying he…" Had he really jumped?

"It would be helpful if you would answer my questions, Riley."

I crossed my arms over my chest. Traveling with Jimmy, I'd spent a lot of time sitting by myself while the band rehearsed or played. Sometimes the band had played big venues, like arenas or halls. But a lot of times they'd played in bars or legions. It seemed like every second place we went, there was someone who wanted to give me a hard time for being a kid in a place that didn't allow kids. Jimmy always told me, *Just because you're a kid, that's no reason for anyone to push you around, and it sure as heck is no reason to let yourself get pushed around. You speak up for yourself when I'm not there.* I got good at speaking up for myself.

"I'm not answering any more questions until you tell me what happened to him."

We locked eyes. He blinked first.

"The chief is going to make a statement," he said, clearly begrudging me every word. "The medical examiner says Ethan was in some kind of altercation right before he died. Do you know what that was about?"

"An altercation? You mean a fight? You think someone pushed him?" He didn't answer. He didn't have to. That was exactly what he was thinking. Either someone pushed Ethan or someone got into a fight with him and that's why Ethan fell. So far, whoever it was hadn't come forward. "It wasn't me."

"You said Ethan texted you because he wanted to ask you something."

"Yes."

"But he didn't ask you?"

"He said he didn't think it was such a good idea to talk about it then and that he'd catch up with me later." But later never came.

There was a knock on the interview-room door. It opened.

"Sorry to bother you, boss." It was Aunt Ginny's voice. "But I think we may have something." She poked her head into the room and did a double take when she saw me. "Riley? What are you doing here?" She turned to Detective Martin. "What's she doing here, Josh?"

"She's being interviewed."

"Interviewed as what?"

"A witness. Someone who knew the victim."

Aunt Ginny crossed her arms over her chest and waited.

"Someone who spoke to him the day before he died," Detective Martin continued. "I'm interviewing everyone who knew the victim. You know the procedure."

Aunt Ginny's eyes darted back to me.

"I—" I began.

"Don't say another word, Riley." She turned on her boss. "She's a minor. You can't interview her as anything without a parent or guardian present."

"She waived the right to have anyone in the room."

"I'm responsible for her, Josh. You know that. You should have told me you were going to question her."

"He said if you were here, it would put you in a conflict of interest," I said. "I didn't want you to get taken off the case."

Aunt Ginny's eyes bored into her boss's. "That's crossing the line. You pretty much coerced her into talking to you alone."

"She signed a waiver." He held up the sheet I had initialed and signed. "And I found this on the roof. You recognize it?" He nodded at the baggie.

Aunt Ginny stared at the four-leaf-clover charm. She said, "Come on, Riley. I'm taking you home."

"I'm not finished with her."

"You are now. She doesn't have to talk to you if she doesn't want to. And she doesn't want to. Come on, Riley. Now!"

I was glad to be able to leave. I didn't want to answer any more of his questions. He was twisting what I said and trying to make me say things that weren't true. He'd said I wasn't a suspect, but he was acting like I had something to hide.

Aunt Ginny grabbed me and pushed me out of the room.

"Wait a minute, McFee." Detective Martin came to the door. "You said you had something. Did the rec-center administrator ID someone?"

"She recognized a lot of kids from the school yearbook. But she can't say which of them, if any, she might have seen go up to the roof that day. Same for the security guard."

"And that helps us how?" Detective Martin said, as if she had wasted his time.

"There's one thing the guard does remember. He says he saw someone come out of the stairwell just after the junior swim meet ended at three forty-five."

Detective Martin dropped his look of indifference. "Can he identify this person?"

"Like I said, the junior meet had just ended. The lobby was full of little kids in rain gear, looking for their rides home. And the stairwell to the roof isn't always clearly visible from where the security guard sits."

"Is that a no, Detective?"

"Whoever it was didn't leave by the front door."

"Oh?" Detective Martin came toward us.

"Apparently, this isn't unusual. The high school kids who use the roof often come and go by a side or rear entrance. He says they're good kids and he doesn't worry about them."

"So he's saying it was a high school kid?" He looked sharply at me. To Aunt Ginny he said, "Perhaps Riley would be more comfortable waiting for you outside with Sarge."

Aunt Ginny didn't respond to that suggestion. Instead she said, "He says the person was carrying something yellow. Bright yellow. He called it neon yellow."

"Something yellow."

"Maybe a raincoat. I'm going to ask around at the school and see if any students have a jacket that matches that description. That is, assuming I'm still on the case."

There was a long pause.

"You're still on it. Good work, McFee."

Aunt Ginny didn't say anything, but I saw a little upturn of her lips—the closest she ever came to smiling (even if it was more of a smirk) when she was on duty. She shoved me ahead of her out of the police station and across the parking lot.

All I could think was: Charlie.

Aunt Ginny drove like a maniac on the way home, which would have been bad enough under ordinary circumstances, but she was driving a police car because her car was still in the shop. Two different people slowed and pulled to the side of the road when they saw her bearing down on them. I glimpsed puzzled and relieved drivers in my side-view mirror as Aunt Ginny whizzed past them without stopping. She was too busy grilling me about why I had been brought in for questioning and what I had said.

I told her everything.

Well, almost everything. I didn't tell her about Charlie's jacket. Not right away.

"You do not talk to another police officer without me being present. I don't care what's going on. Do you understand?" She was finally winding down.

"I understand." I waited a few seconds. "Aunt Ginny, why do you think Ethan had two cell phones?"

She looked annoyed but not surprised by the question. She drove the rest of the way home in silence while I texted Charlie: **We need to talk.**

He didn't text me back. He didn't answer when I called him either.

SEVEN

I texted Charlie again as soon as I got up the next morning. Still no reply. I dressed, grabbed my stuff and rode to his house.

"My goodness, everyone is up and about so early this morning," his surprised mother said when she answered the door. "He left ten minutes ago. He said he had a homework assignment he had to finish for first period."

I raced to school.

Charlie wasn't at his locker. He wasn't in the library either. I roamed up and down the hallways, peeking into classrooms. I even checked the gym, where a bunch of girls were practising gymnastics routines. No Charlie anywhere. I didn't see him until math class, right before lunch.

"Psst! Hey, Charlie!"

Mr. Carver turned from the whiteboard, where he had been writing equations.

"Is there something I can help you with, Ms. Donovan?"

"No, sir."

"Good. Then I suggest you get to work."

I glanced at Charlie from time to time while I copied the equations into my binder. He didn't look at me even once.

I grabbed him as soon as the bell rang.

"We need to talk."

If I was ever asked to describe Charlie, the first thing I would say is that he has a friendly face. A face that usually wears a smile. A face that tells you instantly he's a nice, easygoing guy.

His face wasn't friendly this morning. He wasn't smiling. He wasn't even trying to be nice.

"So talk," he said.

"Not here." I pulled him out of the classroom and around a corner, where it was quieter.

"What do you want?" He looked around impatiently, as if he had somewhere else to be, somewhere more pleasant.

"Why are you acting like that? And why are you avoiding me?"

"I'm not avoiding you. Look, you said you wanted to talk to me. Do you or don't you?"

At that exact minute, I didn't. He was being a jerk. I had to remind myself that he was my friend.

"It's about your jacket," I said.

"What about it?"

"Where is it?"

"What's it to you?"

He was doing his best to make me go away, but I refused to leave. Jimmy always said that if you wanted to get anywhere with people who were all worked up, then the ruder or more obnoxious they got, the calmer you needed to stay. He called it *Bomb Defusing 101*.

I took a deep breath.

"It's nothing to me. But it's a big deal to the police."

"The police? What do you mean?"

"When I ran into you that day, you said you'd seen Ethan. You made a comment about him, something about how charming he was. Did you talk to him, Charlie? When? After school? Were you on the roof with Ethan?"

"Are you accusing me of something?"

"I was at the police station last night. They questioned me about Ethan. When I was leaving, I heard someone"—I didn't tell him it was Aunt Ginny—"say that the security guard at the rec center remembered seeing someone carrying a bright-yellow jacket come out of the stairwell to the roof."

"I didn't wear my yellow jacket that day, so it couldn't have been me."

"Can you prove it?"

"Prove it?" He pulled his head back a little, as if I had insulted him. "Prove what? To who? To you? Or the police?" He was angry again.

I thought back to when I had met him on my bike that afternoon. He hadn't been wearing his yellow jacket. I was positive. But had it been in his backpack? I had no way of knowing.

"The cops think that a yellow jacket or raincoat is the lead they've been waiting for. They're going to ask around, Charlie. Everyone has seen your jacket. Half the kids in school have teased you about it. The police are going to get around to you. They're going to ask you about Ethan. And your jacket."

Nothing.

"Charlie, no one's said anything yet, but the cops…they say Ethan was in some kind of fight just before he died. They think that has something to do with him falling off the roof."

Charlie glanced down at his right hand. Scabs had formed over the knuckles that had been raw three days earlier.

"How did you skin your knuckles?"

"I told you. I punched a wall."

"That's what you told Ashleigh. You told me you fell."

He shoved his hands into his pockets.

"I know you saw Ethan that day, Charlie. You told me so yourself."

He said nothing.

"I also know you're mad at me because of Ethan," I said. "But I had nothing to do with him hanging around me. I still don't know what he wanted. But I was never interested in him, Charlie, if that's what you think. And I don't think you would ever push someone off a roof." Not on purpose, anyway. But maybe, just maybe, if he was mad enough, and it happened that Ethan was standing somewhere precarious...

"Like it or not, though, it won't take long for the police to find out who at school owns a bright-yellow jacket, and to get the security guard to look at a photo array that includes your picture. So if you were up there that afternoon, and if those skinned knuckles have anything to do with Ethan, I think it would be better if you talk to the police before they come looking for you."

"I went up there," Charlie said finally. Slowly. "Right after school. I was hoping to get there before any of the jocks did. But Ethan was already there. He told me to get lost. I tried to talk to him—"

"About what?"

"It's personal. And like I told you, he told me to get lost."

"And?"

"And I did. I didn't have much choice."

"Where's your jacket, Charlie?"

The question became irrelevant as soon as the words were out of my mouth. Looming behind Charlie were Detective Martin and Mr. Chen.

"Your parents are around today, right?" I asked Charlie.

He nodded.

"Call them as soon as you can. Insist on calling them. Don't say anything until you call them."

"Riley, what are you—"

Detective Martin tapped him on the shoulder. "Charles Edison?"

Charlie turned to face him. I felt sorry for him. If he was being taken in because of his jacket, then he was in for a hard time no matter who interviewed him, Aunt Ginny or Detective Martin. First they would ask him about Ethan. If they had managed to locate Charlie based on a description of his jacket, I had no doubt that they had also questioned a few people—kids and adults—about him too. They wouldn't have to dig too deep before someone told them about Ethan and Serena, and me, and Charlie. For sure Aunt Ginny would take note of those scabbed knuckles. For sure she would ask about them. She wouldn't like it if Charlie was evasive. They would make him account for his day—every minute of it. They would pay particular attention when they got to the end of the school day. If he didn't bring it up himself, they would ask him about the roof. Had he ever been up there? When was the last time he was up there? Then they would ask about his jacket. They would want to see it. If he didn't hand it over, they would get a warrant. They would send the jacket for forensic tests—blood, DNA, maybe fibers. They would ask him the same questions over and over, but in different ways, until they were satisfied that he was telling the truth. Or until he could convince them to believe him.

If he could convince them.

I watched Charlie being led away. Then I went looking for Ashleigh.

She found me first.

"I heard the cops just arrested Charlie." Her voice was loud enough to attract the attention of a group of girls nearby. "I heard he was on the roof just before Ethan died."

I shushed her, but it was too late. The girls had heard her and started buzzing to each other. At least two of them were also texting.

"They didn't arrest him." I made sure the girls heard me as clearly as they had heard Ashleigh. "They want to ask him some questions."

"That's not what I heard," Ashleigh said. "I heard he was definitely arrested."

I grabbed her by the arm and pulled her into the girls' washroom, which, fortunately, was empty.

"They didn't arrest him, Ashleigh."

"Melissa Forbes was in the office when the police came looking for him."

"I was with Charlie when they found him. I was standing right beside him. He wasn't arrested. He was taken in for questioning. It's not the same thing."

"But the cops have an eyewitness who saw him on the roof right before Ethan died."

"Who told you that?"

"Are you kidding? Everyone is talking about it, Riley."

"Well, everyone is wrong. All they have is a security guard who says he saw someone carrying something yellow come down from the roof that day."

"Security guard?" Ashleigh frowned. "What are you talking about?"

"What am *I* talking about? What are *you* talking about?"

"Andes. He told the cops he went looking for Ethan after school, but when he got to the roof, Ethan was having a huge argument with Charlie, so he left. He says he doesn't think Ethan or Charlie saw him."

"Aunt Ginny talked to Andes and some other guys from the football team the day it happened. She talked to them again the day after. Nobody mentioned Charlie then." I thought for a moment. Nobody had mentioned Charlie to me. But that didn't mean his name hadn't come up when Aunt Ginny spoke to Andes. It's not like she would have told me if it had. Neither would Andes.

I thought about what I knew. That Charlie had skinned his knuckles and told two different stories about how it happened. That despite all the teasing he'd been subjected to, he hadn't stopped wearing his yellow jacket until after Ethan died. That he had gone up on the roof and had seen Ethan. And that Andes had seen him there. Andes, who, according to the rumor mill, had been pining for Serena and was doing his best to comfort her now that Ethan was gone.

What I didn't know was why had Charlie gone up to the roof? And where was his jacket?

First things first.

"What if Andes is lying?" I said. "What if he had an argument with Ethan over Serena? What if he's getting nervous, so he decided to point the finger at Charlie?"

Ashleigh stared at me. "Andes? I seriously don't think he has enough functioning brain cells to come up with something like that."

"Well, we're going to find out."

"What do you mean?"

"We're going to talk to him."

"We?"

"I don't know where to find him."

Ashleigh did.

Andrew "Andes" Maracle was in aisle six, snack food and soft drinks, at the local supermarket where Ashleigh worked as a cashier. When we got there, he was restocking family-sized bags of potato chips. We watched him for a few seconds from the nacho-chip end of the aisle.

"Well, go on. I thought you said you wanted to talk to him," Ashleigh said into my ear.

Go on? "Aren't you coming with me?"

She looked up the aisle, which was almost totally blocked by Andes's massive body. "Nope. You want to go and accuse The Hulk of lying, be my guest.

But I saw the movie. I know what happens when he gets angry."

I took another look. Andes was at eye level with the packages on the top shelf. He was the human equivalent of the little brick house that the Big Bad Wolf couldn't blow down, no matter how hard he huffed and puffed. It was easy to see how he'd gotten his nickname. He had fallen into a rhythm as he worked, dipping into a huge box, scooping up bags of chips, swinging around to place them on the shelves. I imagined those hands curled into football-sized fists. I imagined the power his whole body could put behind a punch. I imagined a body sailing over a railing high above me.

"What are you waiting for?" Ashleigh hissed. She gave me a little push.

That's when Serena appeared at the other end of the aisle. Andes stopped stocking. He turned to face her, so I couldn't see the expression on his face. But hers was clearly visible. It was pinched into a look of fury. She said something to him that I couldn't hear and then spun around and walked away. Andes dropped the chip bags he had been holding and ran after her. I followed.

He pushed through a door between the dairy display case and the meat counter at the back of the store. I reached the door, but my way was blocked by a man in a green jacket with a store name tag pinned to the breast pocket.

"Employees only." He pointed to the sign on the door. "If you need help with something…"

I ran to Ashleigh and shoved her toward the dairy counter.

"They went out there. Go see what they're up to."

I raced in the other direction, through the checkout counters, out the front door and around the side of the store.

I found Ashleigh outside the rear exit. She was standing alone on the asphalt.

"They're gone."

"What do you mean, *gone*? Did Andes go back to work?"

"I listened to them from the door. They were having some kind of argument."

"About what?"

"I don't know. Serena was telling Andes she was going to do something."

"What?"

"I don't know. He said he didn't think that was a good idea, not now."

"Do you think it has something to do with Ethan?"

"I don't know."

"Where did he go?"

"I don't know that either. But he went with her."

"I thought he was supposed to be working."

"He is. But I saw them go. They went that way." She pointed down the street that ran behind the store. There was no one in sight. "She was really upset."

If she was that upset, it had to have something to do with Ethan. Something Andes knew but didn't want her telling. But what? Did it have anything to do with Ethan's death? If it did, why didn't Andes want her to tell? What, if anything, did it have to do with Charlie?

"I have to talk to him," I said. "And her."

"Andes might talk to you," Ashleigh said, "but Serena? No offense, but not after what she's been posting about you."

"She posted stuff about me?"

"Well, you did steal her boyfriend. According to her, of course."

"I didn't steal him. I wasn't even interested in him. I'm not interested in anyone."

Her eyes popped open. "Not even Charlie?"

"He's my friend."

"That's it?"

"That's it."

"Well, somebody should make that clear to him." She looked pointedly at me.

"I just hope he didn't do anything stupid." Translation: I hoped he had an explanation for his skinned knuckles and missing jacket—one that would satisfy Aunt Ginny and Josh Martin. "Do you know where Andes lives?"

"You don't want to go there."

"Why not?"

"Because it's way out of town, almost in the woods, and it's creepy. His dad runs a junkyard. Well, he calls it a salvage operation. The place is full of old cars, scrap metal, all kinds of stuff. It's surrounded by a fence, and there are two vicious pit bulls guarding the place. You know what pit bulls are like, right, Riley? They go for that hold-and-shake kind of biting. And when they grab hold of you, they don't let go until *they* decide to."

"I don't want to go to his father's junkyard. I want to go to his house so I can talk to Andes."

"The house is in the middle of the junkyard. Inside the fence. Trust me, you don't want to go there. Wait until school tomorrow."

I hate waiting. But I also hate guard dogs, especially pit bulls. They scare me. A lot. I decided to wait until football practice the next day.

EIGHT

I fell asleep soon after that but woke up when Aunt Ginny got home. I found her raiding the fridge.

"There's spicy chicken and noodles," I said. "They're just as good cold as they are hot."

She pulled out the dish they were in, removed the lid and dug in with a fork.

"What happened with Charlie?" I asked.

She sighed. "You know I can't—"

"I just want to know if he's okay. He's my friend, Aunt Ginny."

"They're holding him."

"You mean he's under arrest?"

She nodded.

"His parents have hired a lawyer who everyone says is pretty good. He's going to try to get Charlie released on bail, but I don't know what his chances are. I think if he said that he got into a fight with Ethan and pushed him, but that he didn't mean for him to die, he might get bail with some strict provisions. But he hasn't admitted to anything." She paused. "I'm telling you this because you're his friend, Riley, not because I want you to spread it all over school tomorrow."

I stiffened. "I would never do that, Aunt Ginny, and you know it. And maybe Charlie hasn't admitted to anything because he didn't do anything."

"I can't go into details, Riley, but it's pretty clear he had some involvement—"

"Why? Because someone says he saw Charlie on the roof just before Ethan fell? How do you know that person is telling the truth?"

"That's why we're investigating, Riley. Someone tells us something, and we check it out. If we can get corroboration, we know we're on the right track."

"Corroboration like the security guard who says he saw someone carrying a bright-yellow jacket like

Charlie's? And the fact that Charlie has skinned knuckles and that the medical examiner says Ethan was in a fight before he died, which I assume means he has some bruises or other injuries that didn't happen because of the fall?"

"You're certainly well informed." Aunt Ginny chewed chicken and noodles while she looked me over thoughtfully.

"Charlie isn't the kind of person to settle disputes by fighting," I said.

"That's not what I hear. Charlie is a small guy. He's been picked on all his life by bigger guys like the ones on the football team. Apparently he took a martial-arts course this summer. There are kids, Riley, who have seen him use some of those moves successfully on guys who used to bully him. What if he did that on the roof that day? What if he and Ethan got into it and Charlie tried to use one of those moves, tried to throw him or something, and it went wrong and Ethan ended up falling?" She finished up the chicken and set the container in the sink. "If it went like that, Charlie should say so. At the very worst, it would be manslaughter. He's a minor. Even if he were convicted, he probably wouldn't end up in prison. Maybe a year in detention and a couple of years of supervision in the community. If he keeps quiet, though, it's going to look like he has something to hide. That won't be good. He could end up being charged with murder."

"He can't confess to something he didn't do, Aunt Ginny. Besides, he has the right to remain silent. It's not up to Charlie to convince you or anyone else that he didn't have anything to do with what happened to Ethan. It's up to the police and the Crown attorney to prove that he did—and to prove it beyond a reasonable doubt."

Aunt Ginny sighed. "I know you like him, Riley. He seems like a nice kid. If he's really your friend, you should try to convince him to cooperate with the police. Refusing to talk isn't going to help him."

When I got to school the next morning, there were more kids than usual milling around outside. They crowded the walk leading up to the main doors. Some of them were reading papers that a couple of girls were handing out. Others were watching as a chair was produced and someone climbed on top of it. It was Serena. She was holding a bullhorn.

Someone pressed something into my hand. Ashleigh. She was breathless.

"I've been texting you."

"Sorry. My phone is in my backpack. What's this?" I held out the three stapled pieces of paper she had given me.

"Take a look."

The papers turned out to be a compilation of articles from the Internet. They were all about Coach McGruder and all from ten years earlier. He had been fired from the university where he'd coached a winning team. The reason for the firing was that he'd helped some of the team members get hold of and take steroids, which was against university policy. One article quoted Coach as saying that all he was trying to do was "*level the playing field.*" According to him, even though most universities had strict policies against drug use, including steroids, not all of them enforced their policies. "*When my guys go out on the field,*" he told a reporter, "*they often have to compete against teams that use steroids all the time. It's not fair.*" Those teams had bigger, heavier players who were stronger because of steroids. Included with one of the articles was a short item on the dangers of steroid use: mood swings, trouble sleeping, aggression, high blood pressure, greater chance of injuring muscles and tendons, jaundice or yellowing of the skin, liver damage and an increased risk of developing heart disease, blood clots, stroke and some types of cancer. It made you wonder why anyone would risk so much.

This was more or less the message Serena was shouting out to the crowd. She accused Coach McGruder of giving steroids to Ethan. He had pressured Ethan to use them. Ethan had refused. He had also done his research. He had found out about Coach McGruder's past. The articles she had passed out were ones she had found in her computer's history, and Ethan was the only person besides her who ever used that computer.

"Ethan tried to get Coach McGruder to stop pushing steroids on players. That's why he's dead."

"Prove it!" someone shouted. "Prove any of it." It was Tonka. Andes was standing beside him. He didn't yell at Serena, but he didn't look happy about what she was saying.

"You want me to prove it?" Serena held something up—a plastic bag with a small glass vial inside. It glinted in the morning sun. I strained to get a good look at it. There was a label on the vial, but it wasn't a pharmacy prescription label—I was sure of it. "I found this in the pocket of Ethan's sweatshirt."

A door opened behind Serena, and Mrs. Dekes stepped out, followed by Mr. Chen. Mrs. Dekes focused on Serena.

"That's enough, Serena. Now give me that." She reached for the bullhorn.

Mr. Chen shouted at the crowd to disperse. "The bell is going to ring in ten seconds. I'm sure no one wants to be marked late."

No one moved until the bell sounded. Then, like a drop of ink dispersing in a pot of water, the crowd thinned and vanished.

I was reluctantly heading inside when an unmarked police car rolled up to the curb. Aunt Ginny and Detective Martin got out and made their way to the main doors where Mrs. Dekes was waiting, toe tapping impatiently, for Serena to get off the chair.

"I think we have this under control, officers," Mrs. Dekes said.

"We received a call," Detective Martin said. "Someone said to come to the school if we want information about the circumstances of Ethan's death."

"That was me. I called." Serena jumped down to face the two detectives. "Ethan was being pressured to take steroids. That's why he was acting strangely before he died. I found this." She held out the baggie to Detective Martin. He examined the contents.

"Did you handle this, Serena?"

"I found his sweatshirt in my room." Her voice cracked. "He left stuff at my house sometimes. He was absent-minded that way. I felt something in the pocket. It was that bottle. I took it out of the pocket. But as soon as I realized what it was, I put it in that bag, in case there were fingerprints on it—besides mine and Ethan's. You know, maybe the person who gave that to him."

"Do you know who that person is?"

She launched into her tirade against Coach McGruder. "He must have hidden his past," she said. "Otherwise, Mrs. Dekes would never have hired him."

Mrs. Dekes looked uncomfortable. "Let's discuss the matter in my office."

Detective Martin agreed. He and Aunt Ginny followed Mrs. Dekes and Serena inside. I trailed after them. I needed to get some things out of my locker before classes started.

Nobody concentrated on schoolwork. Everyone was talking about what Serena had said. Was it true? Is that why the team had done so well since Coach McGruder came to the school? Were other members of the team using steroids? Were other teams using steroids? Was Coach right when he said that taking steroids was the only way to ensure fair play, to level the playing field? And then, of course, there was the bigger question: Did Coach kill Ethan to stop him from telling anyone what was going on? If he got fired again for the same reason, his career would be over—permanently.

"You heard Tonka," someone said. "Crawford was the smallest guy on the team. Maybe he decided all by himself to bulk up. Maybe Coach had nothing to do with it."

"Ethan would never do anything that stupid," another kid said. "He was a smart guy. Sure, football was in his blood, but that doesn't mean he'd take chances with his health just to play high school football."

"What if it led to a scholarship?" a third kid fired back. "Do you know how many guys would do anything to get an athletic scholarship or to end up going pro?"

Someone else scoffed. "Steroids or no steroids, Ethan was too small. He was never going to go pro."

As for me, I assumed that, at the very least, football practice would be canceled until Mrs. Dekes could sort out exactly what had happened and who had done what.

I was wrong.

Coach McGruder was on the field as usual. So was the team. Coach didn't say anything about Serena's accusations, and no one asked. He also didn't blow his whistle as often or as loudly. Nor did he yell at any of the rookies or assign extra laps to players who messed up their drills. The minute practice was over, he left the field.

"Poor Coach," Tonka said. "Do you think it's true what Serena said—about him getting fired from his last job, I mean?"

"So what if it is?" Andes asked. "He's the best coach we've ever had. This school has been to the provincials six times since he's been here. We made the national semis twice. You know what Coach always says—*if you're not in it to win it, you shouldn't be in it at all.*"

"Yeah, but what if you only win because of steroids?" someone else asked.

The two veterans turned on the rookie who had spoken. They looked like two mountains turning on a tiny anthill.

"Who asked you, rook?" Tonka said. Side by side, he and Andes advanced on the kid, who stumbled back a step, turned and ran off the field. "Twerp," Tonka muttered.

I hesitated. I was sure Aunt Ginny and Detective Martin would follow up on Serena's accusations. I hoped they would. But Coach could have an alibi for the time Ethan died. Serena could turn out to be wrong about him or wrong about what she had found in Ethan's pocket. For right now, Charlie was still the prime suspect. I couldn't begin to imagine how terrified he must be. I had to do something to help him. I drew in a deep breath and approached the two football players.

"Andes, can I talk to you for a minute?"

He looked down at me. I'd never felt so small in my whole life.

"What do you want?"

Tonka was watching me, curious.

"It's kind of private," I said.

Andes's shoulders heaved in complete indifference. But he nodded at Tonka, who took the hint and wandered away.

"It's about what you told the police," I said to Andes when we were alone. "About what you saw on the roof before Ethan died."

"What about it?"

"Well…what *did* you see exactly?"

His eyes narrowed. "What's it to you?"

"Charlie Edison is my friend. I can't believe he'd ever intentionally push someone off a roof."

"Whatever," he said. "All I know is what I saw."

"Which is?"

He looked me over as if he was trying to decide whether or not he wanted to answer. "I saw what I saw," he said. "You sure you want to hear it, Charlie's friend?"

I nodded. I was pretty sure.

"I was looking for Ethan."

"When was this?"

"You going to let me tell this or not?"

"Sorry. Go on."

"It was right after I got sprung by Cavendish."

"Cavendish. You mean the chemistry teacher?"

Andes crossed his arms over his chest.

"You going to keep on interrupting me?"

"Sorry."

"I got sprung by Cavendish and I went to look for Ethan. I knew he was working out on the roof. He was always working out, trying to bulk up. But when I got to the top of the stairs and opened the door, I could hear right away that he was having an argument with someone."

"Did you see who it was?"

"Not right way. I heard them. Well, I heard Ethan. He was doing all the talking, and he was angry."

"About what?"

"He was telling your friend, *Watch out, or you're going to be sorry.* It wasn't hard to figure out what that was about. There was no way I was going to walk into the middle of a fight over a girl, so I left."

I felt my cheeks color. He was staring at me as if he was trying to understand what Ethan had seen in me.

"It wasn't about me." I don't know why I cared what he thought, but I wanted to keep that straight.

"Whatever. Is that it? We done?"

"You said you just heard their voices. Did you actually see them?"

"You calling me a liar?"

"No. I was just wondering when you saw their faces."

"I didn't have to see their faces. I recognized Ethan's voice, and I saw that stupid jacket."

"What jacket?"

"That yellow one. Makes your *friend* look like a giant happy face. What's with him anyway? Is he color blind?"

"So you saw Charlie's yellow jacket, but you didn't actually see Charlie. Is that what you're saying?"

"It was him. He's the only person in town with such puke taste."

In other words, he hadn't seen Charlie's face.

"You didn't go out onto the roof? You didn't actually see Charlie and Ethan standing together?"

"I just told you—I didn't want to get involved. I backed off."

"You heard Ethan's voice and you saw Charlie's jacket. Was he wearing it?"

"No. He had it in his hand."

"Which hand?"

"How do I know which hand?"

"Think."

"His left hand. He had the jacket in his left hand."

"But you didn't actually see Charlie."

"I know what I saw. Like I told the cops, it was Edison." He scowled at me. "*Now* we're done."

"Wait!"

He loomed over me.

"Do you think Ethan was taking steroids?"

He snorted. "You kidding me? You saw him. Did he look like a guy on steroids?"

"What about the bottle Serena found in his sweatshirt pocket?"

At the mention of Serena's name, his face softened.

"I don't know. I really don't. Maybe he was thinking about taking them. Maybe he was tired of being the runt. He was fast, that was for sure.

And he could kick. But he took a beating every time he was on the field. But even if he was thinking about it—and even if he started taking them, which I don't know—that doesn't mean Coach had anything to do with it."

"Did you ever hear Mr. McGruder talk about steroids?"

"Okay, that's it." He held up a hand. "You're starting to sound like a cop. I got nothing else to say."

He left me standing alone on the field, thinking about what he had said. He was right about what Serena had found. It was a big leap from finding drugs in Ethan's sweatshirt to concluding he must have gotten them from Coach McGruder. But if not from Coach, then from whom? You need a prescription to get steroids, and I knew from some quick online research during my spare period that they were rarely, if ever, prescribed to teens. Besides, there was no pharmacy prescription label on the bottle, which meant the bottle must have come through another channel. Serena had said Ethan was acting strangely before he died. Had that behavior been the result of steroids? Andes had heard him raging at someone. Had it been a steroid-induced rage? Did Ethan have steroids in his system when he died?

And what about that yellow jacket or raincoat? Everyone knew Charlie was jealous because Ethan was hanging around with me. And everyone knew Charlie had a bright-yellow jacket. Maybe someone else had the same jacket. Maybe the cops would find that person—if they decided to look.

I needed to talk to Charlie. I dug my phone out of my pocket and called his mother.

NINE

Charlie had been released on bail and tagged with a GPS ankle bracelet that allowed him to go no more than a couple of meters outside his house before it sounded an alarm that would dispatch the police.

"The nearest youth detention center is down in Toronto," he said glumly. "My lawyer had to argue pretty hard, but he got the judge to agree to let me stay home. They charged me with manslaughter, Riley, and the Crown attorney said that charge could be upgraded depending on how the investigation proceeds. Right now they say two different people saw me on the roof with Ethan right before he died, that one of them heard Ethan shouting at me and that it's obvious I was in a fight. They wanted to take a saliva sample for DNA."

"Did you let them?"

"My lawyer wanted to force them to get a warrant, but I told them to go ahead. I went up to the roof, and I talked to Ethan. But I didn't hit him, and I didn't push him off the roof."

"Why did you go up there, Charlie?"

He shook his head. "It's bad enough I had to tell the cops. I had to tell your aunt, Riley." He let out a long, exasperated sigh. "Whatever. You're just about the only person who doesn't know. You know that four-leaf clover I gave you?"

"About that, Charlie…"

"I took it off your backpack."

I gaped at him. "*You* took it? Why?"

"Because I was mad. Because I thought…because of Ethan. I took it because I thought you were going to get rid of it anyway."

"I would never do that."

"And then, I don't know, I saw him up there, looking over the railing, and he yelled something at me. About my jacket. So I threw the charm at him. I don't think he even noticed. He was gone from the railing by then."

"I was looking everywhere for that charm, Charlie. I didn't want you to think I didn't like it or that I'd been careless."

"I went up there right after school to see if I could find it. Ethan wouldn't let me look. He barely let me through the door. He said he was busy. From the way he was acting, I think he was expecting someone."

"What do you mean?"

"He kept checking his cell phone."

There had been a phone on the roof. Ethan's phone. With the missing SIM card.

"I argued with him, but I didn't get into a fight. I swear it. I left after maybe two minutes. I figured I'd go back another time when he wasn't there."

"If he was waiting for someone and didn't want anyone else around, why didn't he lock the door?"

"It's a door to the roof, Riley. It locks from the inside."

Charlie's story was different from Andes's story. But why? Was Andes lying? Or had he made innocent assumptions about what he had seen?

"How did you hurt your hand? I've heard two different stories."

"I punched a wall. After Ethan made me go."

"What about your jacket?"

"I got rid of it. Geez, when I wore it, everyone acted as if I was committing some kind of fashion crime. And now that I've gotten rid of it, the cops are acting like I committed another kind of crime."

"What did you do with it?"

"I threw it out. I got tired of being teased all the time. A guy can only take so many banana, lemon, bumblebee, traffic light, canary, pee stain—"

"Someone called you a pee stain?"

"That jerk Tonka. So I ditched it. I put it in that clothing-donation box down near the church."

"Did you tell the police that?"

He gave me a withering look. "Of course I did. They sent someone down there right away to get it. They probably want to test it for DNA too. For Ethan's DNA, I mean. But I wasn't wearing it when I was on the roof. I got rid of it before then. I told the cops that. They didn't believe me. Nobody believes me."

"Someone saw a person leave the stairwell carrying something the same color as your jacket. And someone else saw you on the roof with it."

"You sound like the cops," Charlie said. "I told you. I didn't bring it to school that day. I'd already gotten rid of it."

"The person who says he saw you says he went up to the roof to find Ethan. When he opened the door at the top, he heard Ethan's voice. He was angry about something. He also saw your jacket."

"I don't know who you mean, but if someone is saying that kind of stuff about me, I bet it's one of the guys from the football team. And he's lying if he says I had that jacket. He's also lying if he says he opened that door while I was up there. No one opened that door. No one."

"He says he didn't open it all the way. He says he *started* to open it and then closed it again once he realized Ethan was yelling at someone."

"He's lying." Charlie shook his head again. "That door didn't open so much as a crack."

"How can you be sure, Charlie?"

"Because the whole time I was there, Ethan had me boxed in. I thought he was just being a jerk.

Maybe he was. He wouldn't let me past him to look—"
He broke off abruptly and took a deep breath. "He
just wanted me to leave. The whole time I tried to
get him to let me on the roof, he kept looking at the
door, like he was expecting someone. It was making
me nervous, and I kept looking at the stupid door
too. Trust me, it never opened a crack. So if someone
says he saw me—"

"He said he saw your jacket."

"Which, as I keep telling you, I wasn't wearing."
He was annoyed now, probably at having to tell me
the same thing repeatedly. "And anyway, where I
was standing, anyone who opened that door a crack
would have had a perfect look at me. He'd have seen
my face, not my jacket."

"Are you sure?"

"Positive."

"Where were you standing?"

"Ethan had me up against one of the vents."

"What vent?" I asked.

"The one opposite the door. You believe me, don't
you, Riley?"

I nodded. I also wondered how long it would
take to get results from the DNA tests. Days? Weeks?

Longer? And when those results finally came in, what would they show?

"I answered a lot of questions for you. Now you have to answer one for me," he said.

"Okay." I hoped our friendship wasn't about to get complicated. Not now anyway.

"What did he want?" Charlie asked.

"Ethan?"

"You said he wasn't interested in you. Then what did he want? Why did he break up with Serena and start hanging around you?"

"I don't know, Charlie."

"That's not an answer."

"Honestly, I don't know. He didn't tell me. Serena says he changed somehow and he never had time for her anymore. She blames me for that, but I only talked to him a couple of times. And mostly I felt like he was interviewing me."

"What do you mean?"

"He knew who I was. I thought that was kind of strange. I'm new, I'm younger, and he's a star athlete. But he knew stuff about me, and he wanted to know more."

"What kind of stuff?"

"How I figured out what had happened with Mr. Goran and the fire. What my aunt thinks about me getting involved in things like that. What it's like living with a cop. What Aunt Ginny is like. Does she hang around with other cops all the time or does she have other friends." As far as I could see, she didn't have any friends. "If it's true what people say about cop culture."

"It sounds like he was more interested in your aunt and cops in general than he was in you," Charlie said.

Now that I thought about it, Charlie had a point. "Maybe he was. So, you see, I had nothing to do with him breaking up with Serena. And he didn't ask me out, not once. He just seemed to want to know things."

"About cops."

"Yeah." But why?

I met Aunt Ginny forty-five minutes later as she made the turn into the parking lot behind the police station. She lowered her window.

"Sarge told me you were on your way back in," I said. I handed her the extra-large latte, two sugars, that I'd bought for her. She took it warily. "Can I talk to you for a minute?"

She regarded me with suspicion as she sipped her latte but finally nodded.

I ran to get in the passenger seat and closed the door.

"Are you still working on Ethan's case?"

Aunt Ginny handed me her coffee cup while she parked the car. When I gave it back, she took a sip before she said, "Okay, spill. I know you want something, Riley."

"Charlie said you took a DNA sample from him and that you also want to examine his jacket to see if Ethan's blood or DNA is on it."

"You talked to Charlie?"

"He's my friend. How long will it take to get results?"

"That will depend on how long it takes us to find the jacket."

"What do you mean? Charlie said he told you what he did with it."

Aunt Ginny looked warily at me. "He did."

"In the charity clothing box outside the church, right?"

"Right."

"So why haven't you found it?" Oh. "The charity box has been emptied. Where did the clothes go? You have to find out, Aunt Ginny."

She looked evenly at me. "The box hasn't been emptied in weeks."

"So the jacket must have been there."

She shook her head.

"That can't be right," I said. "Someone must have taken it."

Aunt Ginny was silent for a few seconds before she said, "Who would do that?"

It was a good question. One I couldn't answer.

"Riley, you've only known Charlie for a couple of months. So you don't know enough about him to be able to tell whether he's lying or, for that matter, exactly what he's capable of."

This was a point on which Aunt Ginny and I didn't see eye to eye. She was suspicious by nature. It made her a good cop, I guess. The problem was that she never turned it off. A person had to prove himself to Aunt Ginny. There was no such thing as presumption of innocence for her.

"I know Charlie a lot better than you do, Aunt Ginny, and I know what kind of person he is. That's why he's my friend."

"I have to get to the station, Riley. So unless there's something else…"

There was. It was why I'd wanted to talk to her in the first place.

"Did you talk to Andes?"

"Andes?"

"A football player. Andrew Maracle. He's the one who said he saw Charlie on the roof with Ethan. Did you talk to him? Or was it Detective Martin? Because if it was Detective Martin, I don't know if he got the right story, Aunt Ginny. Andes didn't actually see Charlie. He just made certain assumptions based on what he heard and saw."

Aunt Ginny was looking at me through narrowed eyes.

"Forget football players for a minute. How would you know what any witness might have said to the police?" She chose her words carefully, neither confirming nor denying what I had told her.

"Everyone knows. My whole school is talking about it."

"Are you implying that a witness lied to the police?"

"Not lied. Assumed incorrectly. He didn't actually see Charlie up there. He saw a yellow jacket. But he didn't see Charlie's face. He didn't hear Charlie's voice. It could have been anybody."

"How do you know this? Did you talk to this witness?"

"Yes. That's what I'm—"

"Stay out of it, Riley."

"Just think about it, Aunt Ginny. Think about what your eyewitness actually saw."

I slid out of the passenger seat before she could say anything else. I hoped she would consider what I'd said. But I had no way of knowing if she would, which made it impossible for me to stay out of it. Someone had to believe in Charlie, and I had already decided I was that person—despite the fact that his jacket wasn't where he'd said it would be.

I decided to check out a few things for myself. But first I called Ashleigh.

TEN

"I still don't get why we're up here," Ashleigh said. "How can anyone tell what another person saw or heard?"

I located the vent immediately. Charlie had said it was right across from the door to the roof, and, sure enough, there it was.

"Stand right here." I positioned her where Charlie had described Ethan boxing him in. I opened the door to leave.

"Hey, where are you going?"

"Keep glancing at the door," I said.

"Why? What am I looking for?"

"The second you see me opening the door, tell me."

"Okay."

I stood in the stairwell with the door closed. It didn't have a round knob but instead a handle that you had to push down to open. I counted off five seconds and then, as slowly and quietly as I could, began to ease down on the handle.

"You're opening the door," Ashleigh shouted.

"You're guessing," I called back.

"I saw the handle move."

"Were you staring at the door the whole time?"

"You said to watch it."

"I said to keep glancing at it. Charlie said Ethan wasn't staring at it. He said he glanced at it."

"What am I supposed to look at in the meantime?"

"I don't know. But find something and alternate between glancing at it and glancing at the door."

"Fine."

I closed the door again and counted to seven this time. I applied the tiniest bit of pressure to the handle.

"Opening the door," Ashleigh called.

"You were staring!"

"I was not! I was glancing back and forth like you said. It's a big handle, Riley. You can't help but notice when it moves."

"Let's try it again."

Ashleigh sighed. This time I pushed down almost immediately.

"Door opening!" she called out.

I tried a fourth time, much to Ashleigh's annoyance. This time I waited a lot longer. She spotted the movement of the handle right away. I stuck my head through the opening.

"This time—"

"*This* time? How long are we going to be up here?"

"Just another couple of minutes, I promise. And this time, when I open the door a crack I don't want you to call out. I just want to see what I can see. Okay?"

I opened the door a total of ten times—which turned out to be the maximum number of times before Ashleigh lost her patience. Every single time, no matter how tiny the crack through which I looked, I could see her perfectly. All of her. Not just her arm or sleeve or whatever it was Andes said he had seen of the yellow jacket, but all of her. Charlie was right again.

There was no way anyone could open that door and not see who was standing there. But Andes had told me he'd seen the yellow jacket and that was how he knew it was Charlie that Ethan was angry with.

Andes was lying.

"Are you done?" Ashleigh asked.

I nodded.

"Good. Let's get out of here. I have to work on my entry."

"Entry?"

"For the photography competition. You could at least try to remember that I have a life too, Riley."

"But you already took your pictures."

"I know. But I have to go through them and pick the best one and then make sure it's cropped right so that the eye focuses where it's supposed to. You can't believe how many kids enter this contest, Riley. You have to make sure that what you send in is your absolute best and that it captures the theme perfectly."

"I'm sure you'll do great."

"You want to come over and see what I've done so far?"

After what she'd just done for me, I felt I had no choice.

Half an hour later, she turned away from her computer and said, "If you say *uh-huh* one more time while you stare out into space, I'm seriously going to strangle you."

"What?"

"Just as I thought. You aren't paying attention."

"Andes lied."

"You've already said that—a hundred times."

"But why? And why would he say he saw Charlie's jacket instead of saying he saw Charlie? I mean, if you're going to lie, why not go all the way and say you saw the person?"

"Maybe he isn't lying. Maybe all he saw was Charlie's jacket."

"Which Charlie swears to me he wasn't wearing because he had already gotten rid of it." I shook my head.

"Maybe Charlie was wrong about where he was standing."

"He was positive. And he said he kept glancing at that door because he had the feeling that Ethan was expecting someone and seemed anxious about it. But every time I opened that door so much as a tiny crack, you noticed. Charlie would have noticed too.

But he says the door never opened the whole time he was up here."

"Well, someone is either lying or mistaken," Ashleigh said. "Because there's no way they can both be telling the truth."

"It has to be Andes. But why would he lie about Charlie?"

"Maybe you're right. Maybe Andes is trying to frame him. Think about it. Serena and Ethan break up. Ethan starts hanging around you. Andes starts hanging around Serena. He has a thing for her, Riley. He always has. But then maybe Ethan says something or does something that makes Andes think he's going to get back together with Serena. The next thing anyone knows, Ethan turns up dead. Who benefits? Andes. Now there's no way Serena and Ethan can get back together, and Andes can comfort Serena and get close to her that way."

"So long as he doesn't get charged with murder."

"The thing is, we don't know if that's what really happened. If Ethan was planning to get back together with Serena, I mean."

"Maybe he said something to somebody."

We looked at each other.

"Maybe someone on the football team," we said in unison.

"He hung around with Andes, Tonka and Munster the most." I said.

"Then you have to talk to one of them. Tonka or Munster, I mean. If one of them knew, then they probably all knew."

"Which means that Andes would have known. We've already proved that he lied about what he says he saw that day. And someone had a fight with Ethan—a physical fight. That's why the police are saying that even if it was an accident, someone else was involved. It could have been Andes. Okay. I'll try Munster first. I talked to him once before."

"He'll be at the rec center."

"How do you know that?"

"He works out there. Come on."

Sure enough, he was where she said he would be, in the fitness area, jumping rope. Ashleigh led me onto the floor, past sweaty bodies walking, running, cycling and weight-lifting their way to physical perfection. She waited until Munster, in sweat shorts, sweat band and tank top, stopped at the two-hundred count. She pushed me forward. Munster looked down at me expectantly.

"Did Ethan say anything about getting back together with Serena?"

He laughed. "You never quit, huh?"

"Did he?"

"Did someone tell you that, or did you figure it out yourself?"

"So he did?"

"He said she was wrong about him and that there was something he had to do, and after he did it, it was going to be cool. He'd make her see. It was going to be okay."

"He told you that?"

"Yeah, he told us. We're not just teammates. We're friends."

"We?"

"The starting lineup."

"Ethan, you, Tonka and Andes?"

"Right." He glanced at the fitness band around his wrist. "I gotta get back to work."

"Now what?" Ashleigh asked me. "Are you going to talk to your aunt?"

"I already tried." If I was going to get Aunt Ginny's attention, I would need rock-solid information.

Andes knew that Ethan wanted to get back together with Serena. He had already lied to me—and the police—about what he had seen on the roof. I had proved that. What else had he lied about?

"Is Andes working today?" I asked.

"He never does shifts on Friday. That's one of the days he works for his dad. Fridays and weekends. You'll have to wait until Monday if you want to talk to him."

"I need to talk to him now. Come on."

"Come on? As in me and you together?" She shook her head firmly. "No way. I know you think I'm exaggerating, but I'm not. Andes's dad is one of those guys who moved to the country to get away from the city. He served in Bosnia and Iraq. He's more than weird. Everyone says he has PTSD or something."

"I don't want to talk to his dad. I want to talk to Andes. And you know what they say—there's strength in numbers."

"Maybe if we had an army with us."

"How far is their place from here?"

"Four or five kilometers."

"So we could get there by bike?"

"Riley, you're not listening to me. I don't want to go out there. There's no way. Those dogs are vicious. So is Andes's dad."

"Please?"

"No."

"I'll take you out for ice cream later."

"There won't be a later. We won't survive being torn to pieces by those dogs."

"It's not like we're going to rob the place or anything," I said. "The dogs are inside the fence, right?" Ashleigh nodded. "So we can stay outside the fence. Andes can come out and talk to us."

"What if he doesn't want to come out?"

"Then we talk to him through the fence."

"What if we run into his dad?"

"We tell him we want to talk to Andes."

"*We* tell him?"

"*I* tell him. I'll do all the talking. I just want you for a little moral support." Not to mention as a witness to anything I could get out of Andes. A witness would make it harder for him to deny what he'd said. "You don't have to say a word."

"Do I have to stand beside you, or can I stand behind?"

"You can stand behind me."

"I'm going to regret this," she muttered.

"No, you're not. Nothing bad is going to happen. This is real life. This isn't the movies."

ELEVEN

I started to doubt myself when Maracle Salvage and Scrap came into view after approximately four kilometers on a road that changed abruptly from asphalt to gravel about halfway to our destination. The graveled surface made cycling much more difficult. Twice Ashleigh hit a rock and almost toppled from her bike.

We passed the turnoff to the county dump. Another half kilometer of bumping along brought us to a fenced-in swath of land sitting in a clearing that had been made by someone cutting down every tree within fifty meters. Stumps dotted the landscape.

The dogs caught our scent and started barking. And growling. Halfway to the chain link, I caught sight of two muscular, squint-eyed canines clamoring against the chain link, their long, sharp teeth bared. For a split second I made eye contact with one of them. He hurled himself against the fence, snarling and snapping. His partner followed suit. Ashleigh and I leapt back.

"See what I mean?" Ashleigh hissed. "What kind of person keeps dogs like that? A psycho person, that's what kind."

As if on cue, a man stepped from behind a rusted-out pickup truck.

"What are you girls doing around my place?" His eyes were as squinty as those of his dogs. He was carrying a shotgun.

I glanced at Ashleigh. Her face was white.

"We…I was wondering if I could speak to your son, Mr. Maracle," I said.

The man told the dogs to sit. They stopped barking instantly and plunked down onto their butts. "You want to talk to Drew?" he said.

"We go to school together."

"Is that right?" He turned his eyes on Ashleigh. "Looks like something's the matter with your friend."

"She's afraid of the dogs."

"Don't tell him that!" Ashleigh hissed.

Mr. Maracle offered the smallest hint of a grin. "Just the dogs?"

"And you too. I guess because of that gun."

He glanced at it and then back at me. "What about you? You're not afraid of guns?"

"My grandpa had a ranch that we stayed at when he wasn't on the road. He had guns there."

"So you're a country girl." He seemed to like that.

"I'm an everywhere girl. My grandpa was also a musician. He toured a lot. All over the world."

"Musician, huh? Would I have heard of him?"

"Maybe. His name was Jimmy Donovan."

Mr. Maracle's face changed instantly from guarded and scary to surprised and smiling. "*The* Jimmy Donovan? Rockin' Jimmy?"

I nodded.

"I heard he died last year. I'm sorry. Now what do you want with Drew?"

"I just want to talk to him for a few minutes. Is he here?"

Mr. Maracle answered by walking over to a gate and pushing a button. With a loud whirring sound, the gate slid to one side. I stepped forward to enter the compound. Ashleigh stayed put.

"Aren't you coming?" I asked.

"No." She was still staring at the two dogs. Not directly into their eyes. I'd warned her they could see that as a challenge and attack her. She was keeping a watch on them out of the corner of her eye.

"I don't think they'll attack unless they're told to."

"You don't think they'll attack?" She shook her head. "I'll wait here."

"But I need—"

"Or I won't wait at all. You can't make me go in there, Riley. I mean it." Her jaw was set, her entire body was rigid, and her expression was deadly earnest. I walked through the opening alone and shuddered when the gate whirred shut behind me. I was inside with no easy way to get out.

I followed Mr. Maracle's directions and found Andes at one end of the scrapyard between two towering rows of old tires, car parts, metal pieces of various sizes, shapes and sources, geriatric automobiles, rusted-out tractors…anything, I suppose, that might fetch a dollar or two. I didn't know anything about the scrap and salvage business, but it didn't

seem all that lucrative, judging from the condition of the office—a weather-beaten, pod-shaped
camper perched on cinder blocks—and the house,
which was set back near the rear fence and consisted
primarily of faded and chipped clapboard and
mossy shingles.

When I got closer, I saw that Andes wasn't alone.
He was talking to a man on the other side of the
fence. I wasn't 100 percent certain, but it looked
as if the man was pushing something through the
fence. I hung back behind a wall of tires and waited.
When I poked my head out again to take another
look, I found Andes's broad back blocking my view.
All I could see was a sliver of the man's face and
one of his eyes—which was looking right at me.
I dove back behind the tires and waited, my heart
pounding. Who was that man? Why was he talking
to Andes through the fence? Why hadn't he come
in through the front gate, like I had? What had he
pushed through the fence?

I waited.

Nothing.

I heard a sound—*thump, thump.*

I counted to ten slowly and peeked out again.

The man at the fence was gone.

Andes was bent over a massive heap of metal parts. He grunted as he untangled them one by one and threw them to the ground. *Thump, thump.* He was wearing a T-shirt and jeans, and his back was drenched in sweat despite the coolness of the autumn afternoon.

I stepped into the open. "Andes?"

He spun around.

"You again?"

"Your dad said you were back here. He seems like a nice guy. I wanted to ask you something."

He straightened up until he towered over me. He was huge. I thought about Charlie with his ankle monitor, and I plunged on.

"Did you tell the police that you knew Ethan was planning to get back with Serena?"

"What's it to you?" He slapped his forehead. "Right. You and the Lightbulb—"

"But you knew, didn't you? Ethan told you. And Munster and Tonka."

"So?"

"So you were interested in her."

"And?"

I felt like a tiny mouse in the shadow of an elephant who might step on me and squash me at any minute.

"And you must have been disappointed when you heard Ethan was planning to get back together with her."

He stepped so close we were almost touching.

"Is that what you think?"

"All Ethan had to do was say he wanted her back, and she would have gone running."

I hardly dared look at him, but when I did the face I saw was filled with scorn. "That's what Ethan thought too," he said. "He thought that just because he decided he wanted her back, that meant she was going to go back. He thinks Serena and I have nothing in common. He doesn't think anyone could have anything in common with me, because of this." He spread his arms to encompass the scrapyard. "To him, I'm just some ignorant, backwoods mass of muscle with no brains. But he didn't know me. He never did. What he sees—what you see—you don't know anything about it. But if you think I killed him, you're wrong. I didn't. But I could have stopped him from getting killed—do you believe that? I could have stopped that little twerp, and I didn't."

"What do you mean?"

"Like I told you, I went up there to meet with Ethan, only he was having some kind of argument with Lightbulb. So I left them to it. And in case you think I'm lying, Tonka was with me."

He hadn't mentioned that before.

"Did he see Charlie too?"

"No. But he was in the stairwell behind me. I ran into him and his girlfriend as soon as I got free of Cavendish. We went over to the rec center. They waited when I went up to talk to Ethan. Then we went to get something to eat. Tonka and Lina even came into the stairwell. There were little kids everywhere. Tonk didn't come all the way up, but he saw me the whole time. He knows I didn't go out there. I didn't kill Ethan, if that's what you think."

It sounded like a pretty good alibi, unless Tonka was in on it too and would lie to back him up. But, Tonka's girlfriend had been there too. That seemed to remove Andes from the suspect list.

"The cops told me what time Ethan went off the roof. It probably wasn't more than a couple of minutes after I went back down the stairs with Tonka. We were scarfing down burgers by then.

I didn't even know it had happened until Serena called me. She was hysterical. If I'd stayed in the stairwell for another couple of minutes, or if I'd gone out on the roof to see what was going on, this never would have happened. No way Lightbulb could have taken on both of us."

"Wait a minute." I was getting confused. "You said you went to find Ethan right after school." Charlie had done the same. "But now you're telling me you were in the stairwell only a few minutes before Ethan went off the roof. But that didn't happen until three forty-five."

"I said I went up there as soon as Cavendish sprang me. He kept me in after school. You can ask him."

That was news to me. "When you and Tonka and Lina went to the rec center, did you go in the front way?" I asked.

He gave me a sour look, as if the front door was for losers.

"We went in the side, same as we always do."

He bent to his work, effectively dismissing me.

"Andes?"

He didn't bother to look up. "What?"

"Do you think Mr. McGruder is pushing steroids on the team?"

He spun around. "Serena's off base on that. Coach told us about his past. He told us he got fired on account of steroids and that he realized he was wrong. He said it's one thing for professional athletes to decide what they want to put in their bodies and whether the risk is worth the reward. But for kids like us, he said the best thing is to rely on your body, to do your best, eat right, work out, stuff like that. He says we need to learn how to think, too, and that short-term gain isn't always worth the risk, especially if that risk includes premature death from stroke or heart failure."

"So as far as you know, no one on the team takes steroids?"

He looked at me evenly. "You asked me if I thought Coach was pushing steroids. The answer is no, not to my knowledge. I gotta get back to work."

I made my way back to the gate. It whirred into action. Mr. Maracle was sitting on a three-legged armchair outside the broken-down trailer. Both dogs lounged at his feet. He nodded at me. I waved goodbye.

Ashleigh was waiting up the road a hundred meters or so with our bikes.

"Did you get what you wanted?" she asked.

"I'm not sure."

"Well, just so you know, there's no way I'm ever coming out here again. I mean it, Riley."

I didn't argue with her.

TWELVE

It started to rain five minutes after I stepped into the kitchen. It was still raining the next morning when I got up.

"I need to go to the library, Aunt Ginny. I have a group project in history, and my group is meeting there. Can you give me a ride to town?"

"I have to leave right now." She gulped down the last of her coffee and glanced at the clock on the stove. "The library doesn't open until nine."

"I'll go and have a hot chocolate," I said.

"How will you get home?"

"When do you get off?"

"You know that depends on how the day goes."

"I'll call you. I can probably hang out at Ashleigh's until you're off work."

Aunt Ginny dropped me off at the Sip 'n' Bite at seven thirty, where I lingered over a hot chocolate until nine. I was practically the only customer the whole time, probably because the rain was coming down in buckets. My feet were squelching when I got to the library, and my shoes stayed wet all day.

By three o'clock that afternoon, my group-project work was done. I called Ashleigh. No answer. I texted her. Still no answer.

I texted Aunt Ginny too. She said she had a couple more hours of work to do. It was still pouring. I resigned myself to staying put. Half an hour later I got another message from Aunt Ginny. She still had a ton of paperwork to do, but she would take the time to drive me home. An unmarked police car pulled up in front of the library a few minutes later, and I climbed in. The rain continued to pound down.

"People are starting to worry about flooding," Aunt Ginny said. "Apparently the last time it rained this long and this hard, the river overflowed and some kids almost drowned."

She drove slowly, windshield wipers slashing back and forth at full speed, but even then visibility was minimal.

"Are you sure you want to drive back to town in this downpour?" I asked.

"I have no choice." She was straining forward so that she could peer out the windshield in the brief moment between the passing of the wiper blades and the onslaught of rain.

"Aunt Ginny, look out!"

Something was barreling down the road toward us. Something big.

A truck.

It was going far too fast.

It swerved toward us.

"Aunt Ginny!"

Her face lit up in the rush of oncoming headlights. She white-knuckled the steering wheel as she wrenched it to the right to avoid the truck that was careening toward us. I wanted to close my eyes, but I was terrified that if I did, I might never open them again.

The truck's horn tore through the rain. Its headlights blinded me. Aunt Ginny yelled at me to hold tight. The car accelerated and slid sideways.

It slammed into something and heaved up into the air. The passenger side, where I was sitting, landed with a crunch in the drainage ditch alongside the road. The impact lifted me up off my seat. With a *phssst*, the air bags deployed and knocked the air out of my lungs. When I finally looked at Aunt Ginny, her hands were still wrapped around the steering wheel, and the wipers were still beating at full speed.

"What happened?" I asked.

She looked at me, her face ashen. "Are you okay?"

"I think so. You?"

"I think so." She unbuckled her seat belt and started to slide toward me. She had to grab the steering wheel to stop herself. Holding on to it with one hand, she shoved her shoulder against the driver's side door. It was jammed. She maneuvered herself around and kicked it. The door budged. A second, harder kick opened it.

Aunt Ginny climbed out first. Once she was on firm ground, she reached in to help me.

The rain came down in sheets, drenching us. I peered into the darkness and saw red lights in the distance.

"Is that the truck that hit us?"

"It had better be," Aunt Ginny said grimly. "Because if it isn't, I am going to track it down and make sure the driver gets charged with careless driving *and* leaving the scene of an accident." She reached back into the car and pulled the keys from the ignition. She walked around to the back of the car and popped the trunk—or tried to. It refused to open all the way. She shoved in one hand, groped around and pulled out what she was looking for—a flashlight and a rain slicker. She tossed the slicker to me.

"No point in both of us drowning."

I wrapped the slicker around me. It was yellow with green neon letters on the back that spelled out *POLICE* and neon bands on each arm so the wearer would stand out in the dark.

"Stay off the road," Aunt Ginny said. "I'm going to call a tow truck."

I huddled under the slicker and waited. The driver of the truck backed up and jumped down to see if we were all right. His face went white when Aunt Ginny introduced herself as a police officer. His voice shook as he invited us to sit in the cab of his truck while we waited for a tow, and he even produced a couple of towels so that Aunt Ginny and

I could dry ourselves. He apologized over and over again.

"The road is greasy," he said. "I downshifted. I swear I did. But that last curve threw me. This is the first time I've driven this route."

Aunt Ginny didn't comment. She demanded to see his license and registration and wrote all of his information into her police memo book. Her lips were tight and her expression somber. She was in full cop mode—and she was furious.

When the tow truck arrived, I stayed put while Aunt Ginny, taking the police rain slicker from me, went out to talk to the tow-truck operator.

"Are you in trouble with her too?" the truck driver asked me, his eyes on Aunt Ginny.

"Most of the time," I said. "She's my aunt. I live with her."

"Is she as tough as she seems?"

"Tougher."

The driver's already pale face turned paler. "I'm new to this company. I'm on probation. If I get fired, I don't know what I'm going to do."

I felt sorry for him, but I didn't see what I could do. Maybe if Aunt Ginny calmed down…

I also felt sorry for the tow-truck driver who showed up. It was Eldridge, the mechanic who'd had Aunt Ginny's car in his garage for almost a week now without fixing it. I sat in the cab of the truck, where it was warm and dry, and cracked the window just enough to hear Aunt Ginny light into Eldridge. If he was halfway competent, he would have fixed her car by now and she wouldn't have been driving a squad car that had seen better days and none of this would have happened, etc. Her logic was off—who could say whether an accident that happened in one car wouldn't have happened in another? Eldridge slouched miserably, the rain soaking him, until Aunt Ginny had vented enough that he could go about the business of hauling the squad car out of the ditch.

She came back to the truck and climbed up beside me.

"He's going to tow the car back to town," she said. "Then he's going to give us a loaner because he hasn't made any progress on my car. There has to be a better mechanic somewhere in this town."

"Rick Grenier," the truck driver said.

"What?" Aunt Ginny paused in her struggle to free herself from the rain slicker.

"You need a mechanic around here, Rick Grenier is your man. He's first-rate."

"Where do I find him?" she asked.

I could have answered her question, but I decided to leave it to the driver. Rick was Charlie's cousin. That didn't mean he couldn't fix Aunt Ginny's car. But it did mean that if Aunt Ginny knew about his relationship to Charlie, she would probably refuse to go to him when, to my mind, his family background was irrelevant.

Aunt Ginny handed the rain slicker to me. Before she jumped down from the cab, she said to the truck driver, "Follow us back into town and report to the police station. Wait for me there."

We ran through the rain and squeezed into the cab of the tow truck, which smelled, for some reason, like salami. As soon as we were under way, Aunt Ginny asked Eldridge to tell her exactly what was wrong with her car and precisely how much longer it would be in his shop. Eldridge glanced at her, smiling reassuringly.

"You don't have to worry about a thing, officer. Like I told you, I have it under control."

"It's *Detective*," Aunt Ginny said. "And as *I* told *you*, I am *not* satisfied with your service to date."

Eldridge's smile wavered, but only for a second. He came back with an easy grin. "Detective, I promise you I'm going to get that car of yours back on the road in no time, just you wait and see."

"You said that a week ago when I brought it in, and I'm still waiting. As I understand it, you have a contract to work on municipal vehicles. You wouldn't want the police department to be dissatisfied with your work, would you?"

"Dissatisfied? Eldridge never has anything but satisfied customers."

"I'm not satisfied. Just so you know, I'm getting a second opinion."

"A what?" Eldridge turned to stare at her. A car horn blared. Eldridge's head snapped forward just in time for him to see he was about to collide with a car whose lane he had wandered into. He swerved. The whole truck shuddered. Aunt Ginny braced an arm across my chest.

The tow truck straightened out and slowed down. Eldridge's body was stiff. A muscle at the side of his neck stood out like a thick rope as he hunched over the steering wheel, his hands still glued at the two and ten positions. He let out a long, slow breath. We drove in silence, all of us breathing faster than usual at first; then all of us slowing down and letting our bodies relax. It wasn't until we were back at Eldridge's garage and he was about to get out of the truck that Aunt Ginny said, "I'm going to have another mechanic take a look at my car."

"That car is in *my* shop. You can't have anyone do anything without my say-so."

"I can, and I will," Aunt Ginny said. "You're lucky I don't just take the car away and have done with you." She turned to me. "Did you know that some mechanics try to pull fast ones on women? They give women padded estimates. They take their time so they can charge more time for labor. They think women don't know any better."

"Hey, I don't do that. I would never do that," Eldridge said.

"We'll see."

Silence reigned for a few moments. Eldridge's hand twitched on the door handle.

"I can take a second look at that estimate," he said. "See where maybe I can knock off a few bucks. Professional courtesy, for the boys—I mean, for the officers—in blue. How about that?"

"That's totally up to you," Aunt Ginny said. "But I'm still getting a second opinion. And if what he says doesn't match up with what you say, I can promise you that I will be on you each and every day, ticketing those cars parked illegally around your place of business."

"Those are customers' cars."

"That are illegally parked and whose owners, I am sure, will not be pleased to see the price of a parking ticket or two added to their costs."

Eldridge opened his mouth to protest, but Aunt Ginny cut him down with a sharp look.

"I have to go back to work," she said. "There's going to be paperwork to do. Lots of it. I'll call you a cab, Riley." She fished out her phone and made a call. A few minutes later a taxi slid up in front of the garage. Aunt Ginny pressed some money into my hand. I started for the cab. "And take this," she said. I heard a loud ripping sound and spun around. Aunt Ginny was holding the large *POLICE* patch from the back of the rain slicker. It had been held in place with Velcro.

"I don't want anyone to get the wrong idea," she explained as she handed the slicker to me.

I pulled it tightly around myself as I ran for the taxi.

THIRTEEN

It rained most of the night. I know because I was awake almost the whole time, thinking about what Charlie had said, about Ethan, and about who else was up on the roof and what he or she might have been doing there. But it didn't do any good. My thoughts just got more and more tangled. By morning the sky had cleared, but my thinking hadn't.

I made myself some breakfast and rode into town. I was going to meet Ashleigh on her lunch break, and then I was going to visit Charlie.

I was on my way to the grocery store where Ashleigh worked when someone called my name.

It was Aunt Ginny. She was standing in front of Eldridge's garage. She waved me over.

"I thought you'd be interested in my second opinion," she said. "Come on."

She took my bike from me, leaned it against the garage door and led me inside. Rick Grenier was waiting just inside the door.

"I believe you two have met." Aunt Ginny looked at me when she said it.

"Riley, good to see you," Rick said.

"Hi, Rick." What else could I say?

Aunt Ginny turned her attention to Eldridge, who was making a good show of being hard at work on her car. Only his feet were visible beneath it. He walked himself crablike out from under it when Aunt Ginny demanded to talk to him. He rose slowly, muttering something about his knees, and wiped his greasy hands on a grape-juice-purple rag before thrusting one out to greet her. She looked icily at it.

"I'm here for the second opinion we discussed," she said.

Eldridge glowered at Rick, who smiled benignly.

"I have everything under control now, Detective," Eldridge said.

"Nevertheless." Aunt Ginny nodded at Rick, who went over to her car and began his inspection.

"I can have it ready for you Monday morning, first thing," Eldridge said. "I can have a new estimate by this afternoon."

Aunt Ginny's phone beeped. She pulled it out, looked at the read-out and stepped aside to answer. When she returned, she said, "I'm leaving you in charge, Riley. I have to get to work. Rick can tell you what he thinks, and if it doesn't match up with what Eldridge told me, turn the car over to Rick. You got that?"

I nodded.

"You understand that, Eldridge?" Aunt Ginny asked.

Eldridge said he did. He watched nervously as Rick slid under Aunt Ginny's car.

I sat down on an old crate. Aunt Ginny's coffee had helped a little, but a few more hours' sleep would have helped a lot more. My eyes kept fluttering closed. It seemed I'd been there forever before Rick asked me to hand him a light. I looked around and found a caged lightbulb at the end of a long extension cord. I took it to him. It was only after I'd handed it over that I saw the thick cord was smeared with grease. My hand was filthy.

"Eldridge must keep some rags around here somewhere," Rick said as he slid out from under the car and saw my predicament. He scanned the messy garage. "Over there."

I followed his finger to a dingy canvas bag hanging off a hook near an equally dingy sink and reached in to grab a rag. What I got was a handful of chiffon. It looked like part of an old-fashioned party dress. I held it up for Rick to see.

"Figures," he said. "Eldridge does things on the cheap."

"Hey!" said an indignant voice. "I heard that! And I do *not* do things on the cheap. I economize."

I dug in the bag for something stronger with which to degrease my hand.

"By using your old underwear for rags?" Rick taunted.

Eew! I snapped my hand out of the bag.

"For your information, those are perfectly good rags."

Rick contemplated the purple one he was using to wipe his own hands. He picked up another on the floor and shook it out—large pink rose blossoms against a mint-green background. Polyester, I think.

"Where did you get these, Eldridge? The church charity store?"

I thought about the chiffon I had first grabbed.

"The church donations box," I said. "Wait until I tell Aunt Ginny."

"No need for that, young lady." Eldridge held his hands out in front of him as if he were face to face with doom. "And anyway, people threw out those things. I'm just recycling them."

"They donated them to the church. They're supposed to go to the store where they help people who are less fortunate," Rick said.

"Less fortunate? You mean poor!" Eldridge's indignation improved his posture immensely. "I grew up poor. I know what poor people will wear and what they wouldn't be caught dead in. I just take the stuff they don't want and put it to good use."

"So you say." Rick wiped his hands on a rag that hung from the back pocket of his jeans. "Tell your aunt that Eldridge may be slow, Riley, but he's doing an acceptable job as far as I can tell. I have to get back."

I nodded, but most of my attention was on the canvas bag. I stuck my hand in again and pulled out every scrap of fabric inside. And there it was. There were several pieces, all the same, all a blindingly bright yellow.

"Is this the kind of thing you recycle from the church charity box?" I asked, holding up a piece for Eldridge to see.

"Oh sweet Lord, exactly like that." Eldridge shook his head at what I was holding. "That was a jacket, if you can believe it. Who in their right mind would walk around in a jacket that color?"

"Do you remember when you took it from the charity box? I mean, when you decided to recycle it?"

"Sure. I was on my way to work Monday morning, and I needed a resupply. So I saved the church ladies a little time and did some presorting for them."

"In other words, you took a yellow jacket—and some other things?"

"Yeah." He looked plaintively at me. "Are you gonna tell your aunt?"

"You're sure it was Monday morning?"

"I'm sure."

"Can I have this?" The pieces of yellow jacket.

"Be my guest. But whatever else you tell that aunt of yours, you make sure you tell her what Rick just said. Eldridge is doing a good job. A darned good job."

Actually, Rick had said *acceptable* job.

Before I left Eldridge's garage, I pawed through the rags more carefully and dug out more pieces of yellow. One sleeve was missing. So was the collar. But I had enough to be convinced that I had the remains of Charlie's jacket in my hands. Before I turned it over to Aunt Ginny, I wanted my own second opinion. I headed for the recreation center.

"Excuse me, sir."

The uniformed guard, whose name tag identified him as Lloyd McKenna, was on the phone when I stepped up to his desk. He held up a finger. He was well past retirement age and had stooped shoulders, gray hair and thick glasses. I wondered what type of security he was able to provide. I waited for him to get off the phone.

And waited.

He was talking to someone named Al about something that was scheduled for that evening. A poker game, it turned out. Al was bringing the cold cuts. Lloyd himself volunteered a plate of "Jeannie's lemon squares—you know the ones I mean." Only when all the details were settled did he turn his attention to me.

"Can I help you, little lady?"

"I hope so. I'm doing an experiment—it's a school project. It's on memory and age."

Lloyd chuckled. "Well, I guess you've come to the right place. You need a lab rat, and you decided I'd fit the bill, is that it?"

"I need a number of subjects," I said. "And since you're a security guard, I thought you would be a good one. It's part of your job to notice things and remember them."

"That's right. It's always been part of my job. Before I retired, I was a vice-principal at a school down south. Vice-principals have to be on the ball." He had that right. Vice-principals are the chiefs of police in every school. "So are you going to show me something and see if I can remember it afterward?"

"Actually, I want to ask you a few questions about what you've already seen." I pulled out my history notebook, flipped it open to a random page and pretended to read what was written there. "There was a terrible accident here on Monday."

Lloyd's cheery, cooperative face grew somber. "The Crawford boy. A tragedy, if ever there was one."

"The police asked you some questions," I said.

The old guard tensed up. "Well, yes, they did. But I don't know that I can discuss that with anyone."

I smiled sweetly at him. "The police detective who spoke to you, Detective McFee? She's my aunt."

"You don't say!"

"I checked with her. She doesn't have any objection to my questions. You can call her if you want to." I prayed that he wouldn't.

"Oh, I don't think that'll be necessary. If she's your aunt and she cleared it, that's good enough for me. Shoot."

"The police—my aunt—spoke to you about what you saw that afternoon."

Lloyd beamed. "That's right. I told her I saw someone carrying a yellow coat or jacket. Even with all the chaos around here that day—it was the big annual swim meet—that stood out. Is that what you wanted to know?"

"Actually, no." I consulted my phony notes again. "My question is, can you describe the jacket to me?"

He cackled with delight. "Another easy one! Sure. It was yellow."

"Can you be more specific?"

"More specific? It was bright yellow. Is that specific enough?"

"Was it solid yellow? Did it have pockets in it? How many pockets? What kind of collar did it have? Was there a hood attached to it?"

He considered my questions. "Your aunt didn't ask me anything like that. I said bright yellow, and that seemed good enough for her."

"So you don't remember anything else about it?"

"The fellow wasn't wearing the jacket. He was carrying it. I saw it in his hand when he came through the door. I can't say about pockets, but I do know there was no hood. And it had black on the collar and on the cuffs." He thought hard. "Now that you mention it, I think there were pockets because there was at least one horizontal black stripe on one side of the jacket, and I can't imagine what that would be if not trim on a pocket. Yes, sir, a bright-yellow jacket with at least one pocket and black trim. That's exactly what I saw."

"But you didn't see the person carrying it?"

"Not clearly, no. This place was jam-packed for the swim meet. I'm not even sure why the jacket or coat or whatever caught my eye, there was so much going on, but it did. If you were to quiz me on what anyone else was wearing, I'd disappoint you for sure. But I was standing here, and a parent came along to ask for directions, and as I was showing her which way to go, I saw that swoosh of yellow flash out that door over there." He pointed across the lobby to a door marked *STAIRS*. "Like I told the police, I figured it was one of the high school kids who hang out on the roof."

"Great. Thank you. And thanks for your time." I closed my notebook.

"How did I do?" Lloyd asked.

"You did great!" I could hardly wait to report my findings to Aunt Ginny.

I raced outside. I had accomplished something— something big. Three big somethings, as a matter of fact. First, I had proved that Charlie had told the truth when he said he'd dropped his jacket in the church donation box. Eldridge had subsequently raided the box for rags. One of the items he'd taken and ripped to pieces was Charlie's jacket. I had most of the pieces. I doubted Eldridge had cleaned it before ripping it apart. Aunt Ginny could have it tested if she wanted to. She could test it as much as she wanted to, and it would get her no closer to Ethan's killer because, second, the jacket that Lloyd had seen the day Ethan died wasn't Charlie's jacket. Charlie's jacket was solid yellow. It didn't have black trim around the collar, the sleeves or the pockets. Someone that day had been wearing a bright-yellow jacket, but it wasn't Charlie. Finally, Andes couldn't possibly have seen Charlie on the roof that day. Charlie had come and gone before Andes ever got there. And Charlie had ditched his jacket by then too.

I headed around the back of the rec center to cut through the schoolyard next door. It was the quickest route to the police station. I paused on the way to look up at the roof and wondered, for maybe the millionth time, whose head I had seen when I looked up that afternoon. Who had been up there, and how had that person gotten out of the building undetected?

It was so frustrating. There had been more people in and around the rec center that day than there had been for months before that. Yet no one had seen a thing, because no one had had the proper vantage point. You'd have had to be a bird to have seen what really went on up there. And birds don't talk.

That's when I saw it.

I gazed up at it, and I wondered again.

Then I decided on a quick detour.

"Sorry—I can't stay for lunch after all," I told Ashleigh. She'd been waiting for me at a picnic table behind the grocery store.

"Why not? What happened?"

Quickly I filled her in on what I had found.

"You mean Eldridge takes stuff from the charity box?" She sniffed in disdain.

"He calls it recycling. But that's not the point, Ashleigh."

"Still, I'm going to report him. Stealing from the poor is despicable."

"It may save Charlie from going to jail."

She considered this. "So where are you going?"

"I need to talk to Mike."

"Mike? Mike Winters? Are you feeling okay, Riley? You've spent the past three weeks avoiding him. Now you want to talk to him?"

I rode out of town and into farm country and dismounted at the opening to the graveled driveway that ran back a hundred meters or so from the concession road to a Victorian-era brick farmhouse with white gingerbread trim and a wraparound porch. Ashleigh was right. I'd spent weeks avoiding Mike, and now here I was, about to ask him for a favor. What were the chances he'd want to help me—especially when helping me might mean helping Charlie? Mike had been bullying Charlie ever since the two started school. But what choice did I have?

I pushed my bike up the driveway and left it next to the house. I climbed the porch steps and rang the doorbell.

Mike's mother answered. She was small and plump, with gold-frame glasses and a ready smile that faded only slightly when she saw me.

"Riley, isn't it?" There were crinkles around her eyes, but I didn't see any genuine delight in her eyes.

"I was wondering if Mike is home."

"He's probably in the milk house. That's the little building in front of the barn. His father had him rinsing out milk cans."

I gulped. Did that mean he and his father were in there working together? Would I have to face both of them at the same time? My feet were as heavy as blocks of cement as I trudged toward the milk house. I stopped in the doorway. Mike was bent over a milk can, sluicing it with water. I was relieved to see he was alone. He straightened when he spotted me, but he didn't speak. He looked at me with disdain, as if I were a barn rodent he wanted to get rid of as quickly as possible.

"Your mom said you'd be here," I said.

He stared at me, one hand holding a hose and the other a wet rag.

"Ashleigh told me you entered the photography competition."

No reaction.

I tried again. "Is this the first time you've entered?"

He set the can aside to dry and reached for another. "What do you want?"

"Ashleigh said you went to the top of the water tower for your entry."

"Yeah. So?"

"I was wondering if I could see the pictures you took."

"What for?"

Before I could even think of an answer, a man came out of the barn and into the milk house. Mike's father. He got the same look in his eyes when he recognized me as his wife had: *what is* she *doing here?* He turned to Mike.

"When you're done here, fill a couple of bottles for your mother. She's making cakes for the bake sale." He left again without acknowledging me.

Mike shut off the hose. "Why do you want to see my pictures?"

I hesitated. If I told him I was trying to help Charlie, would he be less likely to help me?

"You were on the water tower the afternoon Ethan Crawford died, maybe even at the exact time he fell. There might be something in one of your photos.

You were shooting the whole town from the water tower, right? Maybe you caught something you don't even know about. Maybe you have a picture that shows who was on the roof."

Mike upended a second milk can and set it to dry.

"Have you looked at your pictures?" I asked. "Did you see anything?"

"Do I look like an idiot to you? I'm up in the water tower, and before I even come down, I start getting texts about what happened. What do you think I'm going to do? Of course I looked at them. It's the first thing I did. I knew Ethan. I knew him since we were kids."

Implication: *And you didn't.*

"I'm sorry," I said.

"There was nothing in the pictures. I wish there was. But I looked at those pictures a hundred times. There's nothing."

"Can I take a look anyway?"

He shook his head. "Is it, like, a hobby for you?"

"What?"

"Thinking you're better and smarter than anyone else?"

What? "I don't think that." I was raised to think just the opposite. *Rich man, poor man, they both put their pants on one leg at a time*, Jimmy used to say. *People are just people. Nobody is better than anyone else.*

"Then why do you want to look at my pictures when I just told you I already looked at them and there's nothing there? Don't you believe me?"

"I just want to help—"

"Or do you have some kind of magical powers? You can look at things and see what no one else can see. Is that it?"

"The police think Charlie did it."

"I know."

"But he didn't."

"And you want to help him?"

"He's my friend. You've got nothing to lose, Mike. If you're right—and you probably are—and there's nothing in your pictures, you'll still be right after I look at them. You can say I told you so."

"*Probably*? I know I'm right."

"So can I look at them?"

He looked at the half dozen milk cans he still had to wash. In a weary voice he said, "Come on."

I followed him back to the house, where he showed me into a bright room that had been set up as an office.

"They're mostly on the computer." He sat down in front of a new-looking laptop. I stared at a large color photograph pinned to a bulletin board on the wall.

I stepped closer for a good look. The photograph had been assembled from many shots that together captured a 360-degree view of the town. It was a perfect circle of the terrain around the central point where the photographer had been standing. I recognized some of the buildings.

"Did you take this?" I asked.

Mike didn't look away from the computer screen. "It's my contest entry."

"It's amazing!"

His head bobbed up. "You think so?"

"Yes. Everything lines up perfectly. I know from the angles that it's not just one aerial shot. If it was, I'd be looking at the tops of things. But I'm not." I studied it again. "You really took this from the water tower?"

"Yeah."

"But how did you get it lined up so perfectly? This must be…" I paused and examined the picture again. "…maybe six pictures altogether?"

"Eleven." He stood up and pointed out the different shots. "I tried to keep my feet in the exact same position every time I turned. I had to do the sequence maybe a dozen times before I got what I needed. Then I Photoshopped them like crazy. I think it worked out okay."

"*Okay*? It worked out perfectly." It really had. I was impressed.

"Well, with digital images, you can do just about anything. But you know what I think would be really cool? If I could have done it the old-fashioned way, with an old camera and real film. When you use actual film, you can't check what you've done right away. You have to set it up perfectly and then wait until you're in a darkroom to see how it turned out. I tried not to look at the shots I took until I finished each sequence. But it's too easy, you know? Some of the early photographers came up with amazing stuff with none of the gadgets we have today. They were the real masters."

I stared at him. I didn't think I'd ever heard Mike Winters say so much on any topic at one time. For sure I never would have guessed he was the kind of person who would be seriously into photography. Or the kind of person who knew as much about it as he apparently did, or who wanted to delve deeper into it for artistic reasons. Jimmy always used to say that people were more than just one thing. They were multifaceted, and even if you didn't see all the sides of a person right away, if you gave it enough time you'd be surprised more often than not. He was right—but I seemed to have forgotten that lately.

"Okay, you want to see all the pictures?" He waved me into the desk chair. "Be my guest."

The first thing I noticed was the date-and-time stamp at the bottom of each frame. That made sense. The photographs all had to be taken on the same day, within the same two-hour time period, in order to qualify for the competition. Immediately my heart sank. Although the pictures were taken on the day that Ethan died, they were taken at the wrong time. According to Detective Martin, the cheerleaders had found Ethan at three forty-five that afternoon. Mike had taken a lot of pictures, most of them time-stamped between three thirty and three forty, with a few taken at three fifty. In other words, all of them had been taken immediately before and after Ethan went off the roof.

"Is the clock in your camera right? Did you ever reset it?" I asked.

"You accusing me of something?"

"No. No, it's just that I ran into Ashleigh after school that day. She was getting ready to go out to take her pictures."

"Yeah. So?"

"School doesn't even let out until three twenty. How did you get up the water tower and start taking all these pictures in ten minutes."

"I knew it." Mike threw up his arms. "I knew you were going to find some way to involve me in this, even though I had nothing to do with it. I was up there for an hour, not twenty minutes. Look, you can't just climb the water tower and start shooting, you know. It's restricted. Off-limits. I had to get permission from the municipality. And I had to have someone go up with me—plus I had to wear a harness, which made it harder to do what I wanted to do. And my parents had to sign a waiver in case anything happened to me. They had to agree not to sue the town. And I had to do it on the department of public works' schedule, which meant that I had to get out of school at three to meet the guy who was going to take me up there— after giving me a stupid safety lecture as if I was four years old or something and didn't have a clue what

I was doing. All the pictures had to be taken between three and five. Mine were taken in that time frame. If you don't believe me, you can check with almost anyone—the town, my parents, the school principal, my English teacher. Be my guest."

"I wasn't accusing you of anything, Mike. I was just asking." I turned back to the pictures. Okay, so they weren't going to show Ethan falling or jumping or being pushed off the roof. But maybe they would show someone else on the roof waiting for him, the person Charlie said Ethan was waiting for. Maybe that person had been hiding on the roof when Charlie was there. Maybe that's why Ethan wouldn't let Charlie on the roof. And maybe Charlie's sudden appearance had made him nervous. Maybe that's why he kept looking at the door.

I clicked through photo after photo. Only one out of every nine or ten pictures showed the roof of the recreation center—and at quite a distance. Right away I saw another problem. Part of the roof was obscured. From above and at the angle that Mike had taken the picture, it was impossible to see what, if anything, was behind the structure that housed the top of the stairwell and the door opening onto the roof.

There was also a large square—I guessed and Mike confirmed that it was the heating and cooling system—near the middle of the roof. I couldn't see what was behind it either. These pictures weren't going to help me.

"Nothing, huh?" Mike said. "Can't say I didn't tell you so."

"It was worth a try." I clicked through the last set of pictures, focusing on the time stamp, which had suddenly changed to just after three forty-five.

"Why did you stop taking pictures for a few minutes and then start again?"

"Taylor texted me," Mike said. "She told me what she had heard, so I took a few more pictures. You know, just in case there was something going on."

I stared at one of the photographs. At the parking lot full of kids and parents. And at the figure walking away from one side of the rec center, carrying something in his hand. Something yellow.

"Did you show this to the cops?"

"What for? There's nothing to see. Besides, by the time I took those, the cops were already on it."

I stared at the tiny figure clutching the yellow garment.

"Can you make this bigger?" I asked. He clicked to enlarge the image, but it broke into blurry pixels.

"What are you looking for?"

I went through all of the photos again, looking for another one with the same person in it, maybe one that showed his face.

There were none.

But I already had Charlie's jacket—most of it—for Aunt Ginny. And the security guard's description of the jacket he had seen, which clearly was not Charlie's.

And now this, someone carrying something yellow, something that could be a jacket, leaving the rec center after Ethan went off the roof, long after Charlie had been and gone. Put those two facts together, and at the very least it had to be enough to get Charlie off the suspect list.

"Can you print me a copy?" I asked. "Can you print copies of all the ones you took after Taylor texted you?"

He gave me a quizzical look but clicked on a printer icon. A few moments later the printer spit out all the copies I'd asked for.

"What are you going to do with them?" he asked.

"I'm not sure."

"Is it going to help Charlie?"

Charlie. Not *Lightbulb.*

"I think so. I hope so."

He clicked out of his photo file.

"I have to get back to work," he said. "My dad is a real stickler for chores."

"Thanks for your help."

"Whatever."

"Mike? I'm sorry for what happened in the summer. I thought…" What had I thought?

"You thought I was the bad guy."

"Yeah. And I was wrong. I'm sorry."

He straightened up. "It hit me pretty hard, that whole thing with my grandfather. I was a real jerk."

"And I judged you too quickly. Jimmy—my grandfather—always said it was wrong to judge someone on first impressions. They're almost always wrong."

"Yeah? Then why are people always telling you that you have to make a good first impression?" He smiled. It suited him.

"Good question," I said.

FOURTEEN

I thought about that picture all the way back to town.

Charlie admitted he'd been on the roof that afternoon. But he'd been there right after school, not right before Ethan went off the roof. He'd disposed of his yellow jacket by then too. Eldridge had raided the charity box Monday morning and taken the jacket well before Ethan fell—or was pushed—off the roof.

Lloyd McKenna, the rec-center security guard, had seen someone with a bright-yellow jacket, but the one he described was different from Charlie's. Charlie's jacket didn't have black trim.

So if the jacket Lloyd had seen wasn't Charlie's, whose was it?

Mike's photo showed someone carrying something bright yellow through the rec-center parking lot no more than a couple of minutes after Ethan fell off the roof. I couldn't see the person's face, but I knew it wasn't Charlie.

It wasn't Andes either. He never got close to Ethan that afternoon, and he had the witnesses to back him up—first Mr. Cavendish and then Tonka and his girlfriend.

If not Andes, then who? And why?

Was Serena right? Did it have something to do with steroids?

When I got to town, I went straight to the police station.

"Sorry," Sergeant Evert, aka Sarge, said. "Your aunt is busy right now. She can't be disturbed."

"Can I wait?"

"It could be a long wait, but be my guest."

I sat down on a battered wooden bench and pulled out one of the photos Mike had printed for me. I circled the person coming out the side door of the rec center, and the time-and-date stamp in the bottom corner, and then drew an arrow to the back of the photo, where I scribbled a note for Aunt Ginny to call me. I dug in my backpack for the plastic bag with the pieces of Charlie's jacket in it and took it and the photo to the desk.

"Sarge, do you have an envelope?" I asked.

Just as Sarge swung around to snag a large brown envelope from a tray to his right, the station's main door opened and two uniformed cops came in. One of them paused when he saw me. He was the cop Detective Martin had sent to drive me to the police station. He nodded at me. Sarge broke into a wolflike smile when he saw the officer.

"Ah, Theroux, just the man I was hoping to see." Sarge crooked a finger, and Theroux approached the desk. Sarge extended a hand. "Your paperwork."

"Still working on it, Sarge." He came right up behind me as Sarge handed me the envelope. I could smell the coffee on his breath when he spoke. I scrawled Aunt Ginny's name on the front and slid the photo and the pieces of jacket into the envelope, doing my best to ignore Theroux's prying eyes.

"Can you give this to my aunt?" I asked Sarge. "It's important."

"I'll do it, Sarge," Theroux said. "I have to pass by the detectives' office to write my report."

Sarge held up the envelope. Theroux disappeared with it through an inner door.

"I want that paperwork!" Sarge bellowed after him.

I shrugged into my backpack.

"Not going to wait?" Sarge asked.

"She'll call me." Soon, I hoped. "Thanks, Sarge."

I was unlocking my bike outside when I got a text. **It's Andes. Need to talk to u. Meet me asap.** He gave me a location and ended with **Don't tell anyone.**

I knew Andes hadn't been on the roof when Ethan died. But I couldn't help wondering about Serena's accusations and the shadowy character I had seen pushing something through the fence to Andes. Maybe Ethan hadn't been taking steroids. But he had gotten that bottle from somewhere, and I had the feeling that maybe Andes knew where.

If I had been on the ball, I might have wondered how Andes had gotten hold of my cell number.

FIFTEEN

I rode out to meet Andes at a roadside clearing just past the turnoff to the dump and on the way to Maracle Salvage and Scrap, close enough to be convenient for Andes and far enough away to give him privacy from his father. Someone had built a fire pit in the middle of the clearing and dragged some logs around it for seating. Andes wasn't there yet. I parked my bike and sat down on a log to wait. I pulled out the rest of the photos Mike had printed for me and sorted through them again, looking in vain for another sighting of the man in the picture I had left for Aunt Ginny. I hoped there was a computer program that Aunt Ginny could use to enlarge the man's tiny face. I'd seen it done on a TV cop show, so there had to be, right?

It's funny how you can look at something a hundred times and not see what's right before your eyes. I held the photo closer to my face and remembered what Mike had said when I asked him if he'd given the photos to the cops. No, he'd said. They were *already on it.*

They were already on it.

I was fumbling in my pocket for my cell phone when I heard something—car tires crunching over gravel. Andes in his pickup truck?

The sound stopped abruptly. A moment later a cop stepped into the clearing. Theroux. The cop who had delivered my envelope to Aunt Ginny. The cop who had shown up first on the scene after Ethan died.

"Riley, isn't it? Detective McFee's niece."

What was he doing here? Where was Andes?

"Does your aunt know you're out here?"

"I was just going to call her." I brought my phone out of my jacket pocket.

"Why don't I give you a ride back to town? I'll throw your bike in the car."

He grabbed my bike and started to his car. "Come on."

"No, thanks," I said. I wished he would go away. "I'm waiting for someone."

He frowned. "Out here, all by yourself? That doesn't sound safe."

I fumbled with my phone to find Aunt Ginny's number. Theroux grabbed the phone from me.

"Come on," he said. "You don't want to do that."

"My aunt is going to be looking for me when she opens that envelope," I told him.

He was shaking his head before I finished speaking. "I don't think she's expecting to hear from you until later tonight."

For a couple of seconds I was confused. What was he talking about? Then it hit me.

"You opened the envelope."

"Where did you get that picture?"

That answered my question. It also probably meant he hadn't delivered my envelope to Aunt Ginny. Had he destroyed it? The pieces of jacket were irreplaceable, but I still had Eldridge and the security guard. They would be able to tell Aunt Ginny that they had spoken to me. They'd be able to tell her what they'd told me. As for the photo, Mike had the original on his computer. All I had to do was get away from this man.

He repeated his question. His tone was more threatening.

"That's none of your business," I said.

He shrugged. "It shouldn't be hard to find out. I know when it was taken, and that angle…" He shook his head again. "I should have known you'd be a problem when I saw you out at Maracle's."

So he was the man I'd seen talking to Andes through the fence when I'd gone to the junkyard. It all came together.

"You've been supplying steroids to the football team," I said. It was the only thing that made sense. "Ethan found out it was you. You went up on the roof that afternoon to talk to him. You were there when Charlie got there, weren't you? That's why Ethan wouldn't let Charlie onto the roof to look for my charm." It was also probably why Ethan had kept his eye on the door latch. He was afraid someone else would show up, and he wanted to talk to this cop alone. "He confronted you, didn't he? What happened? Did you get into a fight? Or did you just push him off the roof?"

Thoughts exploded in my head. That man in the photo, walking away from the rec center carrying something yellow. A cop car in the parking lot of the rec center, seconds away from the scene of Ethan's death, but no police car arriving on the scene until well after the ambulance. Ethan asking me about cops. *Do cops stick together? Do they hang out together? Do they protect each other?* Had that been the point of his questions? Had he found out something about a cop? Maybe something about a cop who pushed things through fences instead of handing them over in a straightforward way? A cop who was doing something he wasn't supposed to be doing that Ethan found out about?

The cop who had been assigned to the police car in Mike's picture. The cop who had taken more than ten minutes to respond to a 9-1-1 emergency right next door. There was only one reason I could think of for that. Theroux didn't want the dispatcher to know how close he was to the scene. He must have told someone—a dispatcher, his sergeant—that he was somewhere else. But Mike's photo placed him practically at the scene immediately before the incident. If he was the one who had pushed Ethan off the roof, then by the time he got back to his car and drove away, he would have been no more than a minute or two away when I made my call. It had taken him over ten minutes to show up—well after the ambulance.

Where was Andes? Had he set me up for this encounter? And then I asked myself the question I should have asked in the first place: how did Andes get my cell number?

I bet there were plenty of ways this cop could have gotten it though. For sure it was in Aunt Ginny's file somewhere. Maybe she even had it at her desk.

"You're making it out to be a big thing," Theroux said. "I helped a couple of guys who asked me for help. That's all."

"Is that what you told Ethan?"

"One of the kids saw me at the gym. He asked me. It's not like I was pushing anything. I told him that. I was doing a favor for a couple of kids, and I don't need any hassle because I just came off suspension at my last job and—" He broke off abruptly.

"You killed Ethan."

"It was an accident. We struggled. He fell."

"Then why didn't you come forward?"

He stared at me.

I had no idea what he intended to do, and I didn't intend to stick around to find out.

I glanced in one direction and took off in a completely different one. Theroux grabbed me before I had gone more than a few steps and almost wrenched my arm out of its socket.

He pushed me ahead of him to his car and dragged my bike behind him.

This was my last chance. I remembered what Aunt Ginny had told me to do if I was ever in trouble. *Don't ever go quietly with anyone who means to harm you. Fight back. Most attackers don't expect it, so take advantage of the element of surprise. Bite, claw, stomp, scream. Get away if you can. Run.*

I grabbed the thumb of the hand that gripped me and yanked it back as far as I could. At the same time, I stomped down as hard as I could on one of his insteps.

He let out a ferocious roar, but he let go of me and my bike.

I jumped on my bike. It was too far to ride back to town, but maybe I could make it to somewhere else safe.

The scrapyard.

I pedaled as fast as I could.

It wasn't long before I heard a car engine behind me.

I stood up so I could push harder, and I kept going. I didn't look back, not even when the police car pulled up alongside me.

Theroux nudged his car against me. My bike wobbled, but I didn't fall. Not right away.

He nudged me with the car again. This time my bike fell sideways, and I crashed into the ditch. I lay there, dazed, as the cop car ground to a halt. I heard the car door slam. He was coming back.

I struggled to my feet and ran away from the road, heading for the trees.

I heard cursing behind me. I didn't look back. I kept running.

Something zinged past me. A bullet? Was he shooting at me?

Don't think about that. Don't think at all. Just run. Don't stop.

Don't stop for anything.

I made it into the trees.

I heard footsteps thundering into the brush behind me.

I kept running, leaping over tree roots, dodging low-hanging branches, zigzagging to stay out of his sight but heading now toward something up ahead, toward the glorious sound of dogs barking.

My lungs were burning. I felt like I was going to throw up. I'd never run so fast for so long. I'd never had to.

I spotted something ahead—a fence. I started screaming as loudly as I could. "Help! HELP!"

I heard a gunshot. Another bullet whizzed past me and exploded into a tree, sending shards of bark ripping through the air.

I was almost at the fence. Mr. Maracle's two pit bulls were already hurtling themselves against it in anticipation.

Right behind them was Mr. Maracle, shotgun in hand.

"Help me!" I screamed. "Someone is shooting at me. Help me."

He raised his shotgun and aimed it right at me. I froze.

"Down," he said.

I threw myself to the ground, and a shotgun blast echoed in the woods around me. I stayed down until I saw a pair of boots beside my head.

"You can get up now," Mr. Maracle said. He reached down and pulled me to my feet. "I'm not altogether certain, but I think I just took a shot at an officer of the law."

"I can explain," I said.

"You'd better do just that."

SIXTEEN

Theroux wasn't dead, but he was wounded. He was taken away in an ambulance under the guard of another police officer.

Aunt Ginny and Detective Martin showed up. Aunt Ginny hugged me and looked me over to make sure I was all right. Then she yelled at me for taking matters into my own hands when I should have talked to her. She calmed down when she realized that I had been at the police station—and when she found my envelope and note to her in Officer Theroux's patrol car.

Andes arrived home in his dad's pickup truck. I'm not sure, but I think he might have driven away if his father hadn't gotten to the truck first. I found out later that he was afraid of how his dad would react to the news that he'd been taking steroids.

Aunt Ginny had us all taken to the police station: me, Mr. Maracle and Andes.

Detective Martin interviewed me. Aunt Ginny took care of Andes and his dad. I had to go over my story twice and then endure Detective Martin's questioning on every single point. He studied Mike's photograph. He studied the pieces of the jacket and listened carefully to everything I said about it. This time he took notes—lots of them. He also recorded my interview.

I wasn't let go until after midnight. Only then did Aunt Ginny fill me in on what had happened, but not before she lectured me again for taking matters into my own hands.

"Some of the players were taking steroids," she said. I'd already figured that out. "Officer Theroux was supplying them, making a bit of cash on the side. He knew someone who knew someone. He claims it wasn't as if he had to force the players to take them. That's what they think they have to do to get ahead. Ethan found out. According to Andes,

Ethan tried to talk the players out of taking the drugs. It led to a lot of tension on the team. Bob—I mean, Coach McGruder—started to give Ethan a hard time because of his attitude."

I overheard one of the players say that Coach gave Ethan a hard time.

"Did Coach know about the steroids?"

"He says he had suspicions, but the players involved denied it. Then Serena discovered steroids in Ethan's sweatshirt and found out about McGruder's background. She suspected him of killing Ethan. Andes knew it wasn't true. He tried to talk her out of saying anything, but she was adamant."

That was what Ashleigh had overheard at the grocery store. Andes had been telling Serena that something wasn't a good idea. He hadn't wanted her to go public with accusations about Coach. But Serena had been determined. She held Coach responsible for Ethan's death.

"But Coach wasn't involved," I said.

"No, he wasn't."

"Ethan found out that a cop was supplying the players."

"Apparently."

"That's why he started hanging around me and asking all those questions about cops. He was trying to decide what to do. I think he was afraid that if he went to the police, they would close ranks around one of their own instead of doing the right thing." I shook my head. "He tried to deal with Theroux on his own, didn't he?"

"Theroux isn't talking yet. But we think so, yes. We have Theroux's cell phone records. He made a lot of calls to a number we haven't traced yet."

"Ethan's second phone, the one with the missing SIM card." I bet Theroux had destroyed it.

"Too bad Ethan didn't trust us," Aunt Ginny said. "If he had, he'd still be alive."

"Now what?" I asked.

"At the moment, Officer Theroux has been charged with manslaughter and attempted murder, among other things. That could change, depending on where the investigation goes. If, as he claims, he was acting alone, just supplying a few players, that's one thing. If he was part of something bigger, well, that's another. Given what we have against him, I'm sure he'll cooperate."

"And the players who were using steroids?"

"That I don't know. I imagine that will be up to the school and their parents. Come on, Riley. It's been a long day. Let's go home."

Coach McGruder was waiting in the lobby. He approached us, looked at me and cleared his throat.

"I, er, I wanted to thank you…that is, I wanted" His face turned crimson. "What I mean is, well, I misjudged you. And, well, as far as I'm concerned, the slate is clean." He looked at Aunt Ginny. "And I want to apologize to you too," he said.

Huh? I swung around to Aunt Ginny.

"Apology accepted," she said.

Coach nodded and opened his mouth to say something else but nothing came out. He nodded and left the station.

"What was that all about?" I asked Aunt Ginny.

"It's nothing."

"It's something. Aunt Ginny. He's been giving me a hard time since he first laid eyes on me. And you warned me about him, remember? What's going on?"

"Really," she said. "It's nothing."

"Aunt Ginny…"

"Okay. I ticketed him my first day on the job. He was parked in a handicapped zone. He gave me a hard time. Then he asked me out, and I gave him a hard time. I guess you could say we got off on the wrong foot."

"You should have told me," I said.

"Would it have made a difference?"

I thought about it. "Probably not. In a weird kind of way, getting stuck working for Coach couldn't have happened at a better time."

Aunt Ginny looked skeptically at me.

"It put me close to the football team," I said. "If that hadn't happened, I wouldn't have been able to help Charlie."

"I like to think we would have been able to handle things without your interference," Aunt Ginny said.

Who knows. Maybe she was right.

Charlie showed up at my house the next day before school to thank me for believing him. He dug something out of his pocket—my missing four-leaf clover.

"If you want it," he said shyly.

"Of course I want it." I clipped it to my backpack where it belonged.

Ashleigh was waiting for me in front of the school. "To walk you to your locker," she said.

"I don't think I need an escort anymore," I told her. I had a feeling everything was going to be okay between Mike Winters and me from now on.

"Are you still Coach McGruder's gofer, or are you free after school?"

"Coach let me off the hook."

"Great," Ashleigh said. "So now you're free, let's do something fun."

"She's already doing something fun," Charlie said. "She's helping me buy a new jacket."

Ashleigh raised an eyebrow. "In that case, I'd better come too. You need all the fashion help you can get."

NORAH McCLINTOCK is a five-time winner of the Crime Writers of Canada's Arthur Ellis Award for crime fiction for young people. She is the author of more than sixty YA novels, including books in Seven (the series), the Seven Sequels and the Secrets series. Norah lives in Toronto, Ontario. For more information, visit www.norahmcclintock.com.

ONE

"Riley!" Aunt Ginny thundered. "Didn't I ask you to break down these boxes?"

I poked my head out the kitchen door and found Aunt Ginny in the middle of the veranda. Except for a narrow pathway from the door to the steps, it was filled with empty cardboard boxes and twists of newspaper that I had used to pack fragile items like dishes. In my defense, when it came time to move, I was the one who'd done the packing—all of it, including Aunt Ginny's bedroom, which, by definition, included Aunt Ginny's most personal items. She was too busy finishing up the paperwork on her open cases to help me.

Then, when we got here, I did most of the unpacking. I hadn't got rid of the boxes yet, but it was on my list.

"Take care of it before I get back from work, will you?" Aunt Ginny said before trotting across the yard to her car. I surveyed the cardboard graveyard that was the back porch. It had never bothered me. I had spent most of my life moving around, especially when I was living with my dad's dad, my grandpa Jimmy, we were often on the road with his band. But then Jimmy died and I had to go to live with relatives I'd never even met. My mom died when I was a baby. My dad? He turned into Albert Schweitzer, and if you don't know who that is, maybe this is a good time to look it up. Dad's a medical doctor with an international charity, and he spends almost all of his time overseas, usually in places that are too dangerous for a kid. He spent a lot of time in Darfur. Now he's managed to get funding to set up a hospital in a remote area of Liberia. He emails me when he can.

Going to live with Aunt Ginny (my mom's sister) after Jimmy died was tough. But it was made a little easier by getting to know Grandpa Dan, Ginny's dad. The two of them, plus my uncles Ben and Vince, were just starting to feel like a real family to me when Aunt Ginny got a job offer she felt she couldn't refuse, even though it meant another move for me, this time to a small town.

So now here we were, just the two of us, in a place where we knew no one and no one knew us.

Look on the bright side, Riley, I told myself. *There's always a bright side; it just isn't always what you expect.* That's what Jimmy used to say. One of the things anyway.

And there *was* a bright side.

My new room.

So when Aunt Ginny left, even though I'd intended to do what she'd asked, I decided the boxes could wait. Besides, the evening seemed to stretch endlessly ahead of me. There was plenty of time. I would break down the boxes and stack them neatly after I took another look at my room.

I loved it. It was huge—three times larger than Aunt Ginny's study in our old place, where I'd slept on a pullout bed for more than a year. My new room contained a brand-new actual double bed (with head- and footboards, a huge improvement over the creaky old hide-a-bed in Aunt Ginny's cramped second-bedroom-office) and offered a spectacular view of the rolling meadows and farmland surrounding the rambling Victorian farmhouse Aunt Ginny had rented. It also had high ceilings and gleaming hardwood floors. I was entranced by everything about it, except the color. The walls were a dull and grimy shade of off-white, like cream left out so long that it had crusted over. I'd cajoled Aunt Ginny into buying me some sunny-yellow paint. My plan was to start painting tonight. Maybe even finish painting tonight. Aunt Ginny wouldn't be back until morning. And it was summer. There was no school to get up for. I could paint until dawn, if I wanted to.

I pried the lid off one of the paint cans, dipped in a brush and applied a thick streak of yellow. It looked glorious, like the sun at noon, like daffodils, like summer. It didn't take long for me to forget about the boxes, and begin to transform my poor Cinderella walls into the fair maiden who steals the prince's heart. I didn't stop until I had finished one whole wall, and I paused then only because I was dripping with sweat despite the gentle breeze that I felt whenever I stepped in front of my open window. I was thirsty too. I went downstairs to get a drink.

I stood at the kitchen sink, gazing out the window while I ran the water until it got cold. There was an eerie brightness in the sky over Mr. Goran's place next door. I filled my glass and took it out onto the back porch to see what was going on.

Flames were shooting up into the sky over Mr. Goran's property. It looked like his barn was on fire.

I raced back into the kitchen, grabbed the phone and dialed 9-1-1. I reported what I had seen and gave the address and location as calmly as I could. "On Route 30, west of Moorebridge."

I slammed down the phone and raced outside again. Of all the places for a fire to break out, why did it have to be Mr. Goran's farm?

Mr. Goran! Was he home? Was he awake? Did he even know his barn was on fire? Was he out there now, trying to battle the blaze? Or was he frozen to the spot, flooded with memories and nightmares, unable to move?

I ran across the lawn, scrambled over the fence and raced toward the blaze, yelling Mr. Goran's name the whole way.

Lights were on in his house, but if he heard me shouting, he didn't answer. When I hammered on his front door, it swung open. I called him again.

No answer.

If the door was unlocked, that had to mean Mr. Goran was somewhere on the property. He had to be at the barn. I ran back to the barnyard and ground to a halt when I heard the scream. It was coming from the barn. I heard something else too. Banging.

"Mr. Goran?" I shouted. "Mr. Goran, where are you?"

"Help! Help me!"

The voice was coming from inside the barn. I raced to the door and tried to pull it open, but the latch handle had been heated to scorching by the fire. I yelped and yanked my hand back. It had been burned. I wound the bottom of my T-shirt around my other hand and tried again. The latch wouldn't give. It was stuck.